Acclaim for Colson Whitehead's *Apex Hides The Hurt*

'Of course, anything Whitehead writes is worth reading for the brilliance and originality of his phrasing. But the reason Whitehead's third novel is so moving and worthwhile is that he perfectly nails the tragic/comic nature of our smoothly packaged, hyper-verbal, and strangely stupid times'

Esquire

'Trenchantly funny and moral'   *New Yorker*

'Breathtaking ... It's pure joy to read writing like this ... On almost every page there is a sentence to dazzle and delight'

San Francisco Chronicle

'Savagely funny ... Whitehead makes impossibly nuanced writing look easy. Like all good writing, and good satire especially, *Apex* allows readers to see their world with a new sense of laughable awe, and with it Whitehead proves once again that he is one of the best new literary voices in America'   *Denver Post*

'No novelist writing today is more engaging and entertaining when it comes to questions of race, class and commercial culture than Colson Whitehead'   *USA Today*

Colson Whitehead is the *Sunday Times* bestselling author of *The Underground Railroad*, which won the Pulitzer Prize and the National Book Award in 2016; *The Noble Hustle*; *Zone One*; *Sag Harbor*; *The Intuitionist*; *John Henry Days*; *Apex Hides the Hurt* and one collection of essays, *The Colossus of New York*. A Pulitzer Prize finalist and a recipient of MacArthur and Guggenheim fellowships, he lives in New York City.

COLSON WHITEHEAD

APEX HIDES THE HURT

FLEET
2018

FLEET

First published in the United States in 2007 by Anchor Books
This paperback edition published in 2018 by Fleet

1 3 5 7 9 10 8 6 4 2

A CIP catalogue record for this book
is available from the British Library.

ISBN 978-0-7088-9875-8

Printed and bound in Great Britain by
Clays Ltd, St Ives plc

Papers used by Fleet are from well-managed forests
and other responsible sources.

Fleet
An imprint of
Little, Brown Book Group
Carmelite House
50 Victoria Embankment
London EC4Y 0DZ

An Hachette UK Company
www.hachette.co.uk

www.littlebrown.co.uk

For Nicole Aragi

APEX HIDES THE HURT

ONE

. . .
. . .

HE CAME UP WITH the names. They were good times. He came up with the names and like any good parent he knocked them around to teach them life lessons. He bent them to see if they'd break, he dragged them behind cars by heavy metal chains, he exposed them to high temperatures for extended periods of time. Sometimes consonants broke off and left angry vowels on the laboratory tables. How else was he to know if they were ready for what the world had in store for them?

Those were good times. In the office they greeted each other with *Hey* and *Hey, man* and slapped each other on the back a lot. In the coffee room they threw the names around like weekenders tossing softballs. Clunker names fell with a thud on the ground. Hey, what do you think of this one? They brainstormed, bullshitted, performed assorted chicanery, and then sometimes they hit one out of the park. Sometimes they broke through to the other side and came up with something so spectacular and unexpected, so appropriate to the particular thing waiting, that the others could only stand in awe. You joined the hall of legends.

It was the kind of business where there were a lot of Eureka stories. Much of the work went on in the subconscious level. He was making connections between things without thinking and then, *bam* on the subway scratching a nose, or *bam bam* while stubbing a toe on the curb. Floating in neon before him was the name. When the products flopped, he told himself it was because of the marketing people. It was the stupid public. The crap-ass thing itself. Never the name because what he did was perfect.

Sometimes he had to say the name even though he knew it was fucked up, just to hear how fucked up it was. Everyone had their off days. Sometimes it was contagious. The weather turned bad and they had to suffer through a month of suffixes. Rummaging through the stores down below, they hung the staple kickers on a word: they *-ex*'ed it, they *-it*'ed it, they stuck good ole *-ol* on it. They waited for the wind.

Sometimes he came up with a name that didn't fit the client but would one day be perfect for something else, and these he kept away from the world, reassuring them over the long years, his lovely homely daughters. When their princes arrived it was a glorious occasion. A good name did not dry up and get old. It waited for its intended.

They were good times. He was an expert in his field. Some might say a rose by any other name but he didn't go in for that kind of crap. That was crazy talk. Bad for business, bad for morale. A rose by any other name would wilt fast, smell like bitter almonds, God help you if the thorns broke the skin. He gave them the names and he saw the packages flying over the prescription counter, he saw the greedy hands grab them from the candy rack. He saw the names on the packaging printed over and over. Even when the gum wrappers were bunched up into little beetles of foil and skittered in the gutters, he saw the name printed on it and knew it was his. When they were hauled off to the garbage dump, the names blanched in the sun on the top of the heap and remained, even though what they named had been consumed. To have a name imprinted along the bottom of a Styrofoam container: this was immortality. He could see the seagulls swooping around in depressed circles. They could not eat it at all.

. . . .

Roger Tipple did not have a weak chin so much as a very aggressive neck. When he answered Roger's phone call, it was the first thing he remembered. He had always imagined it as a simple allocation problem from back in the womb. After the wide plain of Roger's forehead and his portobello nose, there wasn't much left for the lower half of his face. Even Roger's lips were deprived; they were thin little worms that wiggled around the hole of his mouth. He thought, *Ridochin* for the lantern-jawed. Easy enough, but at the moment he couldn't come up with what its opposite might be. He was concentrating on what Roger was saying. The assignment was strange.

He hadn't kept up with Roger since his misfortune, as he called it. He hadn't kept up with anyone from the office and for the most part, they hadn't kept up with him. Who could blame them really, after what happened. Occasionally someone reached out to him, and when they did he shied away, made noises about changing bandages. Eventually they gave up. He wasn't expecting the call. For a second he considered hanging up. If he'd planned it correctly, he would have been in a hermit cave in the mountains, two days' trek from civilization, or in a cabin on the shore of a polluted lake when Roger phoned. A place where you can get the right kind of thinking done for a convalescence after a misfortune. Instead, there he was in his apartment, and they just called him up.

He was watching an old black-and-white movie on the television, the kind of flick where nothing happened unless it happened to strings. Every facial twitch had its own score. Every smile ate up two and a half pages of sheet music. Every little thing walked around with this heavy freight of meaning. In his job, which was his past present and future job even though he had suffered a misfortune, he generally tried to make things more compact. Squeeze down the salient qualities into a convenient package. A smile was shorthand for a bunch of emotion. And here in this old movie they didn't trust that you would know the meaning of a smile so they had to get an orchestra. That's what he was thinking about when the phone rang: wasted rented tuxes.

He could almost see the green walls of the office as Roger spoke. Roger's door ajar and the phones on all the desks out there doing their little sonata. If a particular job was really successful the guys upstairs sent a bronze plaque to your office, with the client's name and your name engraved on it, and below that whatever name you had come up with. Roger had a lot of plaques, from before he became a manager, from when he was a hotshot. His former boss came into focus as he listened. He saw Roger tapping his pen, crossing out talking points and notes-to-self as he explained to him how this kind of job wasn't appropriate for the firm because of conflict of interest, and how the client had asked for a recommendation and he was top of the list. It wasn't appropriate for them but they'd take the finder's fee.

There was some token chitchat, too. He found out that Murck, the guy the next office over, his wife had had another baby that was just as ugly as Murck Senior. That kind of stuff, how the baseball team was doing this year. Roger got the chitchat out of the way and started to talk about the client. He had turned the sound off on the television but he could still figure out what was going on because a smile is a smile.

If Roger had called a week ago, he would have said no. He
told Roger he'd do it, and when he put the phone down it came
to him: *Chinplant*. Not his best work.

. . . .

He was into names so they called him. He was available so
he went. And he went far, he took a plane, grabbed a cab to the
bus station, and hopped aboard a bus that took him out of the
city. He pressed his nose up to the glass to see what there was
to see. The best thing about the suburbs were the garages. God
bless garages. The husbands bought do-it-yourself kits from infomercials, maybe the kits had names like *Fixit* or *Handy Hal
Your Hardware Pal*, and the guys built shelves in the garage and
on the shelves they put products, like cans of water-repellent
leather treatment called *Aquaway* and boxes of nails called
Carter's Fine Points and something called *Lawnlasting* that will
prevent droopy blades. Shelves and shelves of all that glorious
stuff. He loved supermarkets. In supermarkets, all the names
were crammed into their little seats, on top of each other, awaiting their final destinations.

The ride was another hour and a half but he didn't mind.
He thought about his retainer, which he had deposited that
morning. It occurred to him that it was an out-of-state check

and would take a few days to clear. Through the window he watched elephants stampede across the sky. As soon as he stepped out of the airport he knew it was going to rain because his foot was throbbing, and now the clouds pursued the bus on an intercept course. They finally caught up when he arrived in the town. The bus kneeled at the curb, he stepped out, and felt the first few fat drops of rain. It rained most of the time he was there, as if the clouds were reluctant to leave after racing all that way to catch him. No one else got off.

The town square was a tiny park boxed by three streets and on the final side by the slow muddy river. A neat little main drag, he thought. It was clear that they were putting some money into it. The red brick bordering the park was recently laid, obviously set down in the last year or two, and there were holes in the ground surrounded by plastic orange fencing where they were adding the next new improvement or other. All the grass in the park was impossibly level. For community service drunk drivers probably knelt with scissors.

People sprinted away from the benches to get out of the rain. They ran into doorways, hid beneath the awnings and over-hangs of the stores lining the square. A lot of the stores seemed, like him, new arrivals. The same national brands found all over. They were new on the first floor, at any rate—on the second and third stories of the buildings, the original details were pre-served, the old-timey shutters and eaves. He imagined crazy aunts in leg irons behind the tiny attic windows of stained glass. In between the new stores, the remaining old establishments hung in there like weeds, with their faded signs and antiquated lures. Dead flies littered the bottom of the ancient window displays, out of reach of arthritic hands.

There was this old white guy in a purple plaid sweater vest who didn't care about the rain. The old guy was walking his dog and taking measured little steps, taking in the activity of the street. He took him for that brand of retiree who becomes a night watchman of the afternoons, patrolling the grounds, scribbling down the license plate numbers of suspicious vehicles. His dog didn't care about the rain, either. It was one of those tiny dogs that had a fancy foreign name that assured you it was quality merchandise. As he talked to the old guy, the dog stood a few feet away and sniffed at a promising stain.

He asked him if he knew where he could find the Hotel Winthrop.

The guy looked at him through the droplets on his bifocals and said, "You're in it, son."

"I know I'm in Winthrop," he said, "I'm looking for the Hotel Winthrop." He extended the piece of paper in his hand. "Number 12 Winthrop Street."

The old guy raised the dog leash and pointed across the park and that's when it really started raining.

. . . .

He said to himself: Bottle a certain musty essence and call it *Old Venerable*. Spray it around the house and your humble abode might smell like the Winthrop Suite of the Hotel Winthrop. The man at registration had told him that President So-and-so had slept there, one of those presidents that nobody has ever heard of, or everybody always forgot was a president at some point. Board of Ed types were always a bit dismayed when they needed to name a new high school and realized that all the favorite workhorses were taken, and were forced down the list to the sundry Pierces and Fillmores. As he looked around the room, he had to admit that it was quite possible that one of those so-and-so presidents had stayed there, after a listless stump speech. It was a good place to make a bad decision, and in particular, a bad decision that would affect a great many people. Considering the nature of his assignment, his quarters were appropriate.

The people of bygone days had pulled dark wood in wagons to panel the hotel walls, and now it was scraped and splitting. They had ordered red-and-orange carpet from the big city catalogs and laid it on the floor for a hundred years of feet, and now it was gauze. The armchairs, tables, and writing desk had been moved so often that the furniture legs had scraped fuzzy white halos into the floor. If he put the three lamps together, he could partially reconstruct the sylvan idyll described on their round bodies—alone, they were too chipped and defaced to relate anything more than ruin. Brittle brown spots mottled the lamp shades where the bulbs had smoldered, mishap after mishap. The previous guests had left their mark. The only thing unscathed through these accumulated misadventures was a painting that hung on one wall. Closer inspection revealed it to be a portrait of one of the Winthrop elders. Winthrop stood in a field with some hunting dogs, preserved in his kingdom. Guests came and went, guests registered, retired, and checked out, but this man remained. He never blinked.

He was relieved that it was not one of those eyes-follow-you paintings. He had recently weaned himself off Drowsatin and didn't want to go back to using it again.

The clients had left some things for him on the wooden desk. Mayor Goode had sent up a bottle of port, Mr. Winthrop had sent him a local history written by a town librarian. Writing your town's local history was the librarian version of climbing Everest, he figured. And Mr. Aberdeen had faxed him a welcome to their fine community, informing him that he and the mayor would meet him in the hotel bar at six o'clock. There was nothing among those things to tell him that they had agreed to his very specific conditions of employment. He frowned and looked over the room once more. He wasn't even sure if he should unpack. The coat hangers were handcuffed to the closet, as if they had been warned in advance of some rumored compulsion of his.

He limped around the room. He was on the top floor of the hotel and had a nice view of the emptied square. He pressed his palms to the sill. People had umbrellas now, not the compact-click found in major metropolitan areas but favorite umbrellas that they never lost, and they made a break out of doorways for their cars or homes, confident now that this was not a brief sudden shower but a rain that was going to hang around for a while. It was a bad cough that had turned into something that showed up on X-rays. The leaves fled one way, then another. From the window, the river along the square was a brown worm without a head or tail. The wind changed, and he was startled by a gust that threw spray against the panes for a few vicious seconds. The bed was safe, well-pillowed, and he made his retreat.

He had an hour and a half to kill, time he could have spent reading up on the town, perusing the information they had sent him, but he wasn't officially on the job yet so he crossed his arms and closed his eyes. Any second a nap might creep up on him. Naps had passkeys to every room in the world, the best kind of staff. He was in the Winthrop Suite of the Hotel Winthrop on Winthrop Street in Winthrop Square in the Town of Winthrop in Winthrop County. He didn't have a map of the area, but he told himself that if he ever got lost he should look for the next deeper level of Winthrop, Winthrop to the next power, and he would find his way.

.   .   .   .

He lost his balance as he entered the hotel bar and almost fell, but no one saw him. The room was empty, the bartender's back was turned. He cursed himself. It would have been a bad first impression to make on a client. He often lost his balance, thanks to his injury. From time to time he could find no sure footing. It always reminded him of stepping onto a broken escalator. A little shock when things weren't moving as they should, a stumble into surprise, a half a dozen times a day. But no one ever saw it because he rarely left his house these days. As he picked out a table, he told himself, no more mistakes. Just a few minutes 'til curtain.

He tried to figure out what was going on in the framed cartoons along the walls, but the punch lines were over his head. Portly Englishmen with round, curved bellies huddled in taverns and drawing rooms referring to minor scandals of their day. He didn't know what they were talking about: I HAD A MINOR WIGGLESWORTH. What the hell did that mean? The chair sighed beneath him. It was an intimate place, twelve leather chairs and three small glass tables. The deep carpet drank all stains. No neon Budweiser signs, no popcorn machines with greasy yellow glass. The salesmen in town for the convention would be perplexed and scurry to their rooms to call their wives.

They were an odd couple, coming through the door, and surely his clients. The woman wore a light blue pantsuit and smart black shoes. She smiled to the bartender and approached in dignified business strides: Regina Goode, the mayor of the village. He reconsidered: maybe it wasn't a business stride and power charge, but the walk of someone who had recently lost weight and was feeling the confidence of her new body. He had seen data from the focus groups of the then-unnamed StaySlim in the marketing phase and felt he knew what he was talking about. And that had to be her favorite perfume, he decided, the smell summoned gold script etched on small crystal, a spritz or two before she dashed out already late to her first pressing appointment of the day. Two syllables. Iambic, natch. He stood and shook her hand.

The white guy was Lucky Aberdeen, founder and CEO of Aberdeen Software, and he came in his costume. The jeans and polo shirt were standard issue, but the vest was the thing, his trademark was a fringed leather vest spotted with turquoise sequins on one breast that described the Big Dipper. It was familiar from TV, from the cover of the guy's book, which had been a best-seller a year ago. He learned later that people in town called it his Indian Vest, as in "There goes Lucky in his Indian

Vest," and "I said hello to Lucky in his Indian Vest." Details from a magazine profile came back to him. Lucky had spent some time in the Southwest after he dropped out of a fancy northeast school, and there on his back in the desert, among the cacti and scorpions, squinting at the night sky, he had formulated his unique corporate philosophy. Lucky tipped two fingers, index and middle, in greeting to the bartender and took a seat. "Hello, friend," he said.

"Thanks for coming down here on such short notice," Regina said. She laced her fingers and rested her elbows on the tiny surface of the table.

"Sorry for the rain," Lucky said, "although sometimes a little rain is nice."

He mumbled in response and nodded.

"Well," she said, clearing her throat, "I trust you've had a chance to review the material we sent."

"This is quite a unique situation you have down here," he said. Understatements were a new hobby of his.

Lucky said, "This is a unique town." Lucky chuckled and Regina tightened her fingers. They were trying to stick to the script, he gathered.

"I still don't understand how you came to this point. Don't think I've heard of a law like this before."

His clients glanced at each other. The mayor cleared her

throat again. Lucky said, "The wording of the law itself is a bit Byzantine, but the idea is still, it's still on the books. It may be from a different time and a bit complicated, but the spirit of the thing is timeless."

"Why not just have the town vote on it?" he asked. "Get it all done out in the open?"

"There are a lot of complications on that point, but I can assure you that we're not circumventing. You see it's the town council that handles the routine matters of law here, and there's three of us—me, Regina, and Winthrop. When we all come together it's a beautiful thing, but when we disagree—"

"A vote wouldn't work in this situation," Regina broke in, "considering the community these days and their concerns."

Yes, he was definitely picking up on a little tension. Which one had the better hand, and who was on the verge of folding their cards? The bartender brought the drinks over without making eye contact. The man could hear everything and he wondered what the bartender thought. This citizen.

"We want to be fair," Lucky said, "is what I think Regina is getting at. We have a lot of longtime residents here, obviously, and they think one way, and then we have a lot of people who have moved here for the business opportunities, they want to raise their families in a nurturing environment." Lucky took a sip of his Brio, the energy drink that had become the late-night lubrication of choice in Silicon Valley. The beverage was Lucky's way of saying that he was not so far in the boondocks that he was out of touch.

"The town is changing quickly," Regina said.

"Right," he said. Behind her head, the caption of a cartoon went, PIP I DARESAY! PIP!

"Rapidly growing," Lucky said. "What we have is a kind of stalemate, and we want to be fair. So we called in a consultant."

And there he sat. He nodded. He wondered, are they seeing the man I want them to see? That devil-may-care consultant of yore? His hand was a fist on the table. He imagined a wooden stick in his fist, and attached to the end of the stick was a mask of his face. He held the mask an inch in front of his face, and the expressions did not match. He said, "I sent an e-mail to someone's office, I can't remember who, about the conditions of my employment."

"Yes, your conditions."

"That's what we wanted to talk about."

"There's some disagreement about the strict terms, but we'll work it out."

"They're a bit binding."

"That's the point," he said.

They looked at each other. Lucky said, "You see, Albert Winthrop's unreachable until Wednesday. He has a boat race.

But I'm sure we'll work it out, once the three of us sit down. I think what you're saying makes perfect sense, if you look at it through the right lens. Perfect sense."

"Will you be okay until then?" Regina asked. "Your room is nice?" She smiled, by accident it seemed to him.

He raised his eyebrows and nodded eagerly. It wasn't that bad a smile, as far as smiles go, a rickety ark sailing above her chin.

"I know Winthrop sent up a few books for you to familiarize yourself," she added.

"And when you meet Winthrop," Lucky added, "I'm sure he'll lay a bunch of family history stuff on you." He chuckled. "He has all this stuff in leather binders."

"I use Apex all the time," Regina said, sitting back in her chair. She wiggled a finger for proof. "Burned it on the stove."

"Oh," he said.

"Quite an impressive client list you have," Lucky said. "Had a question about one thing, though, if you don't mind. It said there you did Luno, but Luno is pretty old, right, it's been around for a long time."

"New Luno. I did New Luno. I added the *New*. They were a bit adrift, demographics-wise."

"Ah," Lucky said, considering this. "New Luno. My nephew drinks that by the crate."

There you have it.

.   .   .   .

He had a limp from an injury. What happened was he had lost a toe recently. Didn't lose it really. It was cut off with his consent and put in one of those red hospital biohazard bags. He'd seen such things on television, and what do they do, he wondered in the hospital, burn the waste in incinerators? His toe consumed by flame and wafting like a ghost through the atmosphere. Of course sometimes medical waste washed up on the shores of public beaches and there was a big news thing about it. The derelict waste-removal company. Now and again he pictured unlucky bathers. That thing they thought was a baby fish nuzzling their thighs in the surf? It was his lost little brown toe, roaming the seas in restless search of its joint.

They say you can get used to losing a toe. And he had to agree, it was not up there on the list of truly terrible injuries. Of course his socks looked funny to him. Balance-wise, the toe is not that essential and it had been brought to his attention that his limp was psychosomatic. But there he was limping.

.   .   .   .

He lingered in the bar after the mayor and the magnate left. They hadn't yet agreed to his stipulations so he wasn't officially on the job, and this comforted him. He lingered over his beer. For a time, cobwebby foam in thin tendrils along the inside of the pint glass was entertainment enough. No one else came in. At one point he heard sounds from the registration area, luggage wheels losing the silence of carpet as they hit the wooden floor, and elevator doors opening and closing. Then silence again.

Wednesday, he thought. Two days. He forced himself to admit that he was a bit relieved. It was the first assignment he'd taken since his misfortune and he didn't know how things would play out once he started working again. He had this suspicion that all he had inside himself now were Frankenstein names, lumbering creatures stitched together from glottal stops and sibilants, angry unspellable misfits suitable only for the monstrous. Names that were now kin.

The bartender ran his cloth across nonexistent stains on glasses, lipstick that had not remained and specks that had not lingered. A streak of gray started at his forehead and fanned out into his Afro in a curly wedge, an ancient and hardwired pattern, in his genes. He watched the man wipe glass, hold up glass to the light to consider his handiwork. The day the bartender discovered that white spray in the mirror, as he was about to perform the daily trimming of his muttonchops, he knew he had become his grandfather, that he was truly his father's son beyond what the surname said. It was hard not to notice that the bartender had some old-school muttonchops, real daguerreotype shit, something to aspire to. He went up for a refill and the bartender spoke for the first time since Regina and Lucky had left. The bartender said, "You come down here to clean up this mess?"

"I'm here to check things out and lend a hand if I can," he answered. He sat down on one of the stools.

"What kind of business do you do?"

"Consulting."

"*Con-sulting*," the bartender repeated, as if his customer had added some new perversity to the catalog of known and dependable perversities.

"I'm a nomenclature consultant. I name things, like—"

"Hell kind of job is that?" The bartender put both his palms down on the bar. He looked like he was preparing to vault over it and throttle him.

He fell into his standard explanation without thinking. Just like old times. "I name things like new detergents and medicines and stuff like that so that they sound catchy," he said. "You have some kind of pill to put people to sleep or make them less depressed so they can accept the world. Well you need a reassuring name that will make them believe in the pill. Or you have a new diaper. Now who would want to buy a brand of diaper called *Barnacle*? No one would buy that. So I think up good names for things."

"People pay you for that shit?"

He was at a loss. He'd kept up a good front for Regina and

Lucky, but he couldn't muster the necessary reserves at that moment. His foot throbbed in phantom pain.

Muttonchops looked him over. Finally, the bartender said, "This is my home."

"Oh, I know that, people live here. They called me in for a helping hand," he said. Already this job was different. Time was, you christened something, broke the bottle across the bow, and gave a little good-luck wave as it drifted away. You never saw the passengers. But there were always disgruntled passengers out there, like Muttonchops. It was simple mathematics.

To be challenged like this, in this strange town. Might as well have his boss hovering over him, inspecting his every notion. And he was long past having any use for bosses, even before his misfortune. It was unpleasant. *De-escalate, de-escalate,* he told himself. A sign behind the bar offered, TRY A REFRESHING WINTHROP COCKTAIL—SPECIAL OF THE HOUSE. He pointed. "Uh, what's that taste like?"

The bartender gave him a look and started toward the bottles.

"Quiet in here tonight."

The man behind the bar huffed and said, "People are getting in tomorrow for the conference," then paused for a moment to glare at his customer as his hands tipped in jiggers. The bartender grabbed bottles of stuff he'd never heard of. The labels were yellowed and peeling, the script on them saloon-ready: the kind of stuff they break on the bar at the start of the brawl in Westerns.

"What's the conference?"

"More people coming in to talk to Lucky about business opportunities. He's always bringing people in here," Muttonchops said. "They're all over the place now." Inside the cocktail shaker some sort of process was happening. "That's what I thought you were here for, until I heard you talking to them."

"Time of prosperity."

Muttonchops snorted. "That's what Regina says. That's what Lucky says." The bartender dropped a cherry into the yellow drink. The red reminded him of the time he broke open an egg and saw something inside that might have lived. "Winthrop Cocktail," the bartender said.

"What do you say?"

"I say, I say I've worked here ever since I was a boy. Used to have a shoeshine over in the men's and that's where I got my start. Like my father and his father. And then they moved out here, behind this bar. They were bartenders behind this very bar and now I'm here, too. My family goes back to the first settlers."

"Wow." He took a sip.

"This was a colored town once," he said. "Founded by free black men and women, did you know that?"

"No." One look at the faces on the walls of the room told him that it must have been a long time ago. Minor and major Wigglesworths, and all points in between. "I read something about barbed wire," he said.

"*Barbed wire.* That was later. No. This here was founded by free black men. They came from Georgia and set up here and built themselves a new life. It was after that Old Man Winthrop came here with his factory and put it on the map. He came here after."

He wondered what was in the drink. He'd only had a few sips and his head was already heavy, his neck a little rubbery. He wanted to blame it on jet lag, but he'd only traveled one time zone over. No, he was suffering his usual case of ST. Standard Torpor. This was more human contact than he'd had in months. And also, he had to concede, the Winthrops really had their magic potions down pat.

"You know how old this hotel is?" the bartender asked. In a moment the man's face had softened. He could no longer say that Muttonchops looked angry, but he couldn't name the man's new expression either. "One hundred and thirty-two years old," the bartender said. "Other places out on the street there, they close. You see them close and some new store opens up in their place. Some of the old-timers, they've had that store for years. They can use the money and retire. Wouldn't sell out for all the money in the world a few years ago but they look up and down the block and they can see what's coming. So it's changing. But this place isn't going anywhere."

"What do you mean?" For a second he thought the bartender was referring to the hotel, but of course there was something more.

Muttonchops shifted on his feet. "Regina's a good woman. I voted for her. I'll vote for her again. Our families, we're intertwined. But what they're trying to do. This is Winthrop. Always will be Winthrop. Shit around here never changes. You can change the name but you can't change the place. It stays the same."

It all swam.

He had limped in. He staggered out.

. . . .

He had no purpose, he had no vocation. He had a job, which he lost, and so he answered the ad in the paper. The advertisement did not use the words *nomenclature consultant* because the big men upstairs knew that the esoteric is often scary. So the ad promised the chance to get in on the ground floor of an exciting new field and left it at that. With the red pen he had stolen on his last day at his last job, he circled the ad. Here's to new beginnings.

It was a midtown job so he told himself first thing that if he got the job it would only be something to tide him over until he got a more permanent gig. Midtown. Midtown the abstraction was nightmare enough, bat-winged and freaky. To actually set foot in the place was almost too much for his mind to process. He had a certain temperament. But he put on some midtown clothes and showed up at the appointed time.

It was one of those buildings where there was one bank of elevators for one half of the building and another set of elevators for the other half. It was hard to escape the idea that the world of the elevators not taken was better, more glamorous, with butlers and canapés and such. He pushed in glass doors. As he waited in reception, his future colleagues walked past, up and down the halls. They were on the inside and he was not. Where were they going, where did that corridor lead? It was the last time he would experience mystery in that building.

After a while he was taken to the conference room. Abe Appleby, the lowest man on the totem pole, the latest hire, asked him if he knew what a nomenclature consultant was. He told him he didn't, and Abe shrugged and told him it was a fancy way of saying they thought up names. Then he left him alone with the aptitude test.

The test was odd. On one of the sheets there was a smiling bear flailing its paws on a pyramid and they asked him to name it. There was a nonthreatening androgynous blob with vague limbs and they asked him to name it. A sleek television-type pastel object, a bicycle built for three, a children's ball that looked like it had a little tumor bulging out of it. A subsection of pills—there was no telling what they did, what ailment they alleviated or cured. He filled in the blank spaces.

There were normal everyday things with pretty much fixed names that they asked him to rename. This is an octagon. What would you call it? More things: stapler, ashtray, tree. The hardest thing was the chair, but he filled in the blank spaces.

Then to reverse it, they gave him a list of product names and asked him to think of what they might be attached to, a fruit drink or a running shoe. It was all pretty obvious stuff. He put in things off the top of his head. When he was finished, he dropped the test in a big pile of other tests on the receptionist's desk.

He went home. Before the evening news he loosened his tie and drank beer out of a can.

They called him in the next day.

He sat in Roger Tipple's office for the first time. Roger observed him over the neat divide of the desk. He picked up his aptitude test and nodded. Then he said, "You're a Quincy man. What year?"

They talked about the old school for the next twenty minutes. Their conversation was facilitated by the fact that the same deathless geezers who had been around during Roger's time were still wheezing around during his time. As luck would have it. He was a Quincy man, and it turned out the firm had been founded by Quincy men. The name meant something. He fit right in.

.   .   .   .

He suspected the Winthrop Cocktail supplied many aliases, but the one he found most compelling was *Sleep*. This passport led him places. For a time. When he blinked and twitched awake at two in the morning, he knew he'd be up for hours.

Caught in the a.m. in a hired room. He roused the man at the front desk after fourteen rings, hoisting the handlebar receiver to his ear. It was one of those old telephones that was all classy curves, white with brass trim; somebody had probably received news of Lincoln's assassination through it. The man at the registration desk said he'd send up the only thing he could make at this hour: a cucumber sandwich.

Travel had rumpled his clothes, sleeping in them had left him hamperish. Groggy, paste-mouthed, he imagined he waited for an audience with the king. He carried urgent dispatches for the man in charge. The royal crest was everywhere, on the ashtray, on the brittle ballpoints and the stationery, the sheets and the towels. Upside down on the cover of the Guest Services folder, the gold Winthrop *W* was the McDonald's *M*. Let us summon the graduate students to study the recurring theme of the golden arch in nature.

In college he had lived next to the Winthrop Library, so when he initially heard the name of the town, his first association was of shelves and shelves of the Classics, the histories of the dead, what we needed to read in order to become real citizens of this country. Then came images of mummified white people and their staggering approach, parchment tongues aching to rasp *Winthrop*. Then: a brand of tooth polish used before World War One, a patent medicine popular before the government cracked down on certain excitatory ingredients. He turned the idea over in his head and decided that if he were to put the name to contemporary use, it would be for a new kind of loofah, a commercial brand, one for institutional use in retirement homes. Scrub that dead skin away.

He let the guy in when he heard the faint double knock. If Muttonchops had started out as a shoeshine boy in the men's room, this was the man who had screwed the shoeshine stand into the bathroom tile. He had obviously been haunting the hotel for a while. As the white man heaved the cart across the carpet, his bones creaked and cracked so much that they sounded like kindling catching fire. Well, we all have our boulders to push up mountainsides, he thought. The man called him sir, and he tipped him. The sandwich lay autopsied on the plate, crusts excised, cut into triangles, leaking horseradish.

He wondered if he could do what they were asking of him. There was still a chance he might get off the hook if they didn't agree to his stipulation. It was simple, albeit a tad unusual. If the clients were going to hire him, they had to let the name stand for a minimum of one year. They could change it after that, but only after a year had passed.

When he composed this little fine print, his intention was that it would force them to consider the process—his process—with the appropriate gravity. These people were not his usual corporate clients. Corporate clients knew the rules of the game, and it was rare that they refused to accept one of his names. Oh, it happened occasionally that a client lacked the necessary imagination, or suffered from long-standing character deficits, or maybe there was some backroom intrigue that suddenly put this or that project on hold. In a case like this, however, especially when dealing with such a green group, the chance of encountering that random X factor was considerably higher. The object in question was a town. There was family and clan to think about, and their bickering. There was heritage and history involved, and their inscrutable demands. It simply made sense. He was a pro, they had called him in for a reason, and he did not want to waste his time.

As he sat on the edge of the bed, hunkered over the cart, it occurred to him that by forcing such exacting conditions on his clients, he hoped to use their refusal as an excuse. To hide his fear behind the impassive façade of the uncompromising professional. The sad shake of the head that said: I have a list of principles. By removing the possibility of failure, he could return home to his convalescence rooms and continue to sulk, pretending that he still possessed his power. Word would get back to the firm and his colleagues would say, Man that guy is tough.

Before they adjourned, he had asked the mayor, "How am I supposed to come to a conclusion?"

And she said, "Do what you usually do. You're the expert."

He had traveled abroad. In European hotels he watched European TV and on it European commercials. Be a tourist, walk the narrow streets, see one old church you've seen them all, but the commercials. It didn't matter if you didn't understand the language, a good name cut through. Does it sound like candy, does it sound like perfume, does it sound like a fancy car you would like to be seen in. These things cut across cultures. In European hotels he could get five countries' programming in five different languages but it felt like home because he understood the names.

He had never seen a cucumber sandwich before. He was in foreign territory but the television brought him back, reassuring his ears with the common roots of their languages. He turned on the television and ate his cucumber sandwich a triangle at a time. And he felt better, sitting there with the sound off, as the light entwined itself along surfaces like blue vines. When he was finished, conditions or no, he unpacked.

. . . .

He had a new desk and a couple of new ties. He was on time and pretended to go-getting.

He got into the swing of things. New guys like him worked in teams. The top guys, the wage earners, worked solo, but most of the jobs were executed by teams, around a big desk in one of the conference rooms, and they brainstormed. They huddled over the material the client gave them, they sipped mineral water and sent people for doughnuts. Perhaps there was a slide of the particular thing projected on the wall so they could see it right there before them in its frustrated glory, and one of the team would lazily guide a laser pointer around contours. Sometimes a representative of the aluminum company or tampon company or manufacturer of plastic wedges might show up to explain matters in person. What it was and where they were trying to go. These representatives were too earnest, got on their nerves, threw off the rhythm of the meetings. There was a rhythm to the meetings. They got into a fever and testified, shouting out the words of imaginary languages, the names of polystyrene gods and Day-Glo deities. The contributions were doomed or had tiny imperfections and they kept going until they came up with the right name.

At first he kept his mouth shut because he still saw the job as an interim gig. He wasn't cut out for corporate life. He believed himself to be of a different caliber than those men. Jocky white guys. He didn't need the same things. The cheap posturing. The signature colognes. The obscure wafting. They scrambled and wanted to be heard by the men who wrote performance reviews and determined bonuses. They wore suspenders. So he sat and watched and whatever names he had he kept to himself. He listened. And if what they came up with was terrible, was prosaic, or even more unforgivable, something else's name, he figured that's the way things work in this crazy job. No skin off his back. Their hapless little creations flopped around like fish on asphalt and he couldn't care less.

But the names. After two weeks of listening he was full of them. Every day the door cracked another half inch and he could see beyond the tiny rooms he had stumbled around in his whole life. He pictured it like this: The door opened up on a magnificent and secret landscape. His interior. He clambered over rocks and mountain ranges composed of odd and alien minerals, he stepped around strange flora, saplings that curtsied eccentrically, low shrubs that extended bizarre fronds. This unreckoned land of his possessed colors he had never seen before. Flowers burst petals in arrangements never considered by the natural world, summoned out of dirt like stained glass. These beautiful hidden things scrolled to the horizon and he walked among them. He could wander through them, stooping, collecting, acquainting himself with them until the day he died and he would never know them all. He had a territory within himself and he would bring back specimens to the old world. These most excellent dispatches. His names.

He couldn't keep them to himself. He started out slow in the meetings, half mumbling the names. They got lost in the general mad chatter. At first it was not important to be heard. It was enough to merely utter the things, let them out. No one noticed and it was fine. After a time he would get a nod here and there at some contribution, and he projected a little zone around himself, a place of low pressure in the room where the rest of the team could expect a certain kind of weather. He gathered force. Then one day after a meeting, Mike Viedt put a hand on his shoulder and said, "Nice job in there." Two meetings after that, instead of holding back, he halfheartedly tossed a name into the hurly-burly, nothing special, to the usual lack of response. Ten minutes later Mike said the name, offering it to the team as his own, and it stuck. They ended up giving it to the client. Mike took all the credit. And he felt—it was fine. He had a million of them in his territory. What had he lost? An unspectacular weed.

He was changed, though, he could not deny it. The next

project they had, he discovered the name right off, he was sure it was the name, and he bided his time. There came a lull, there were always lulls. As one of the guys scrambled after the takeout menus so they could haggle over lunch options, he slapped his hands on the table. Not too loud, but enough to draw their attention. They assumed he was going to lobby for Thai. They looked at him and he said it: *Redempta*. It was the name. It stuck. They got paid. Not long after that he got his own office. He had to admit, it was pretty cool.

.   .   .   .

The sun crept up, he heard some Main Street morning friskiness down below, and he finally fell back to sleep. He was busy battling various guised things in a dream he would not remember when he was awakened by a loud shriek.

"Housekeeping!"

The door threatened to splinter under her fist. "Housekeeping!"

He quickly looked around, but neither saw smoke nor smelled fire. Nor did he hear hotel guests running in the hall outside, robes tugged tight against their chests. No emergency, then. He mumbled, then repeated himself with more volume: "I'm okay!"

"I need to get inside!" the voice wailed. It sounded as if

she were throwing her shoulder into the door. No, something heavier. Her cleaning cart.

"I'm okay!" he shouted once again.

"You should be up by now!" the woman thundered, and then all was quiet. Was there something he was supposed to do? He waited, and soon he heard the woman push her cart up the hall. After a few long minutes, he slipped his hand outside the room and noosed the doorknob with the DO NOT DISTURB sign, which featured a moody silhouette of sheep jumping over a fence. He noticed thin daggers of paint on the floor that had been knocked loose by the assault.

He dressed and limped over to see the Admiral. After his sleepless night, he needed a familiar face. It was not the first time he had been saved by the recognizable logo of an international food franchise, its emanations and intimacies. No matter what time zone you happened to be in, the Admiral's doors pushed in with the same slight resistance, freeing the vapors of the latest excursion into Africa, South America, or Blend. He listened to the sound of the brewing machines, their staccato gurgling. It was black gold bubbling from the earth's crust, the elemental crude. He approached the teenagers with a smile, and they smiled back. All over the nation teenagers served the sacred logos and he thanked God for the minimum wage. Who knew what kind of havoc the restless servants of Admiral Java might unleash upon the world if they cast off their yokes.

They kept the plastic surfaces clean and everything was plastic. The shop was so immaculate that it looked like it had opened yesterday, but if someone pulled out a photo from 1872 showing palominos tied up in front, he would not have suspected monkey business. A degree of fastidiousness was a big part of the franchise agreement, one of the deep and numerous responsibilities of those in Admiral Java's family. They had to stick to the rules if they were going to use the name. Even the farthest colony received weekly newsletters from HQ outlining the specials, the recent hairnet edicts, the latest volleys in the great sanitizer debate. Any customer might be an emissary from the home office come to check compliance, register corruption in tiny boxes on legal-sized paper. Spies were everywhere. My limp is a weak disguise, he said to himself. The medium Sumatra arrived superbly. He dropped audible dimes into the tip cup.

This was the world he moved in, a place of compacts and understandings. It was safe in that embassy. He knew how things worked again. Steam snaked out the sip hole. He commandeered one of the people-watching stools in the window and found that dangling there was more comfortable than the four-poster bed he had slept in the night before. Across the square he saw the dark entrance of the Hotel Winthrop, the frosted glass, the somber gleam of brass in the sick light. The rain had diminished and redoubled through the night, wishy-washy, and now murmured to a drizzle. But he knew it was going on for a while. His foot continued to throb. Since his misfortune he had a farmer's ken and understood weather arriving.

Behind the window of Admiral Java, peeking past the name stenciled on the glass, he was able to take a more accurate survey of the town's makeover. They had the new computer chain, the sneaker chain, the convenience-store chain, Admiral Java of course. Affirmations of a recognizable kind of prosperity and growth. More than half of them were clients of his (former) firm. If he had not suffered a misfortune, his heart would have swelled. He would have been the grandma stooping in her garden to check on how the tomatoes were coming along. Instead he had to settle for a recollection of pride, and heat through the recyclable container.

In between the chain stores and the old stalwarts, he found representatives of that contemporary brand of establishment, the kind that dressed itself in rustic sincerity but adhered to the rapacious philosophy of the multinational. They were easily spotted despite their camouflage. The homey flower shop run by women in long dresses who had forced out the previous mom-and-pop operation, the pricey home-furnishing store where expense crouched behind the subterfuge of calligraphic price tags, the restaurant that had changed hands but maintained the fifties furnishings and quaint original signs for the kitsch factor. *Old-fashioned* was a name after all, he had attached it to a new brand of lemonade or pie on many an occasion. The Hotel Winthrop was not the only holdout of what had been, but from his vantage point on the swiveling Admiral's stool it was the axis. The tallest building on the square, the looming accusation.

They were even getting an Outfit Outlet, so he was implicated. At the end of the block, a brick two-story building was quarantined by blue plywood. While he couldn't make out the letters on the posters along the fence, he knew what they said. COMING SOON OUTFIT OUTLET. The familiar stacked O's were the giveaway, the slim ovals in the infinity configuration. If you didn't recognize it, they had failed. Walk five blocks in any major city and you were bound to come across an Outfit Outlet. He had named the store a few years back. The parent company was a successful purveyor of low-priced low-quality goods that had decided it wanted a different piece of the action. So the same sweatshops stitched together flashier clothes from the same fabrics, and midwifed profit. The new member of the corporate family was doing well, due in no small part to the name, of course. Of course. Not that the work they did was shoddy. It was hard to walk into an Outfit Outlet and not find something, even if it was a lowly sock, that did not serve a purpose in your wardrobe or the persona you connived to project to the world.

It was nice when he thought something up and the marketing people ran with it, coming up with an appropriately smart logo or campaign or tagline or something that looked nice heaving on T-shirts. In the case of the Outfit Outlet infinity design, the marketers had even displayed a sort of coy self-consciousness about the business of the franchise. Whether everybody was in on the joke or not, it was hard to argue with a cotton T.

Would they demolish the old building rather than preserve the façade? No stopping the double O. They grew up fast. Such things happened in a blink, the things you name go on without you. Had the fence been there yesterday? He couldn't remember. He felt reduced again, half erased. Instead of being comforted by the familiar stores and reliable logos, they reminded him that this was the longest he had been out of his house since his misfortune. When he left Winthrop in a few days, the store would probably be open for business, with the mandated pop CDs on shuffle, that month's colors laid out for discovery of *your size*. Some people drive miles to watch foliage; he had heard of people who made regular pilgrimages to the windows of Outfit Outlet to watch the colors change.

Maybe that last part isn't true, but it should be.

. . . .

Muttonchops saw him cross the threshold and poured a draft. He supposed the bartender wanted to let him off easy, after having witnessed the quick damage wrought the night before by the Winthrop Cocktail. When he reached for his wallet, the bartender sneered or appeared to sneer and informed him that everything was on the house, per instructions. The bartender nodded to the portrait of a Winthrop elder on the wall in confirmation, per his tic. The dust on old Winthrop's face did not stir. Something still consumed the founding father's attention outside the frame after all those years, a loping fox or an escaping slave. No, he corrected himself: there weren't slaves this far west—the bartender himself had told him that the town had been founded by freed slaves. So it had to be something else. He tipped Muttonchops a buck. When he left the bar later, the dollar was still there, and one or two more, and for all he knew the bartender dropped them in the garbage once he was out the door.

The day had drained away without incident. He'd had his coffee and returned to his room, noting happily that the DO NOT DISTURB sign had kept the place free from intruders. He napped to the sound and flicker of a twenty-four-hour news station. There had been a bombing, and retaliation. No word

from his sponsors. He ate dinner in his room and declared it
cocktail hour.

Outside the bar, the lobby was busy with talk of names and
how many nights, as tired pilgrims leaned at reception to deliver
credit cards to the world of incidental charges. The quiet of the
previous night was at an end. No more fretful scanning of the
horizon; this ghost ship had found the shipping lanes again.
There were six other patrons. They sipped and squeezed limes
into their drinks and commented on the accommodations and
the journey. Talking about details, giving them a hearing, helped
tame the loss of beloved routine. Someone asked, "What time is
it there?" The slang of everyday exile, of in-between places like
airports and hotel bars.

He tried to figure out how old the coasters were and what
sort of maintenance they required. Did human hands scrubbing
attain that faded suppleness, or did dishwashers achieve it easily
with a switch? A spray from an aerosol can, the name of it
pointing to both the scientific and the traditional. Apply *Weathertique* for that lived-in look that will make your house into a
home. Also a verb. Did you Weathertique the chair yet, dear?
Too many syllables, he decided. He felt a bit Weathertiqued
himself.

It did not take long for the couple sitting next to him at
the bar to interrupt his noodling. Jack and Dolly Cameron.

He'd overheard them talking about houses they'd passed on the way to the hotel, as they formed from exteriors conjectures about interiors that might meet their needs. Behind that window or that one was a family room, surely there was room for a home office and a place for visiting in-laws to sleep twice a year. The man addressed the side of his face. "You here for the Help Tour?"

"Help Tour? No—"

"Not everybody's here for the conference, Jack." She smiled.

"It's a natural question," her husband snapped. She looked down at her drink and he continued, "Everybody in here is on some kind of business. Why else would they be here?" Jack returned his attention to him. "What's your line of work?"

"Consulting."

"What kind of consulting?"

"I'm a nomenclature consultant. I name things like new cars and toothbrushes and stuff like that so that they sound catchy. You have some kind of insurance policy to reassure people or make them less depressed so they can accept the world. Well you need a reassuring name that will make them believe in the insurance policy. Or you have a new breath freshener. Now who would want to buy a brand of breath freshener called *Halitotion*? No one would buy that. So I think up good names for things."

"Wow," Dolly said.

"You're here about the town's new name," Jack said. "Heard about that."

He nodded. Jack wore khaki pants and a blood-red sweater. White collar erupted out of the V-neck. How did they skew, the demographic of two sitting next to him? He wrote the script: Jack had responsibilities, he was climbing the ladder, but was trying to hang on to some notion of the youth rake. On Saturdays he put on his old college sweatshirt and hunkered over the papers he had to get through by Monday a.m., as if putting on sweats could take the sting out of working on the weekend. There were stains from his glory days, from poker marathons and touch football. The detergent was never what it was cracked up to be and Jack was grateful for that, because those stains were reservoirs of hope, and cherished as such, ac-counting for all those lost years.

Dolly was also decked out in the national khakis, accented by a seaweed-green blouse. A small string of pearls cupped her neck, and when her husband said something that diminished her, she ran a finger across the pearls to reaffirm their presence. Perhaps she did this to remind her of his affection, perhaps the necklace was an asset she might pawn one day as part of her exit strategy. According to the script, she had a full-time job, nine to five, but outside the nine to five there were hormonal hours, and she cocked her ear to their little ticking. Thus her earnest talk about bedrooms, and how far away the kids' rooms should be and the system of who would get out of bed to soothe on what days of the week. Jack drank scotch, Dolly nursed a vodka tonic. He had no idea what a Help Tour was at that point, but he liked the name.

"Winthrop sounds nice," Jack said. "Sounds distinguished. I mean look around this bar, the history. But I think Lucky is up to something with his idea. I mean this is the twenty-first century. Sometimes you got to catch up with what's going on." His watch clinked as Jack rested his arm on the bar. It was an expensive watch, and made its way into the script: poking out of the sleeve of his sweater, it told Jack what he was working for, and what he had achieved.

"It is a homey little place, though," Dolly said. "We came a day early to look at property," she informed him, grinning away.

"I'm not saying it's not a nice place to raise kids, honey. I'll tell you, brother, where we are now, the housing stock has gone through the roof. We go out to see a place from the newspaper—"

"—or our realtor drives us out there—"

"—and what you're getting for the price is a damn bungalow. There are these retirees who try to get ten—"

"—twenty—"

"—times what they bought their houses for thirty years ago. Move to Florida with that money. But for a couple like us—"

"—bedroom for each of our kids and a guest room at least—"

"—it doesn't make any sense."

Muttonchops offered his back to them, obviously eavesdropping despite the occasional cover gesture, smearing a cloth across a glass, turning labels on bottles face out. He wondered what he would have made of their little back-and-forth if he hadn't been looking into their faces, cataloging every twitch. Their tag-team wrestling match with the domestic world. It was in the little gestures that he found the true meaning of what they were saying, in what their hands darted toward, in how their eyebrows and lips tilted, dipped, and scurried about their faces. It was there he saw the honesty.

In the old days, these were his Great Unwashed, the clueless saps who came to his names and connotations seeking safe shores and fresh starts. Try This, it will spackle those dings and dents in your self. Try New and Improved That, it will help keep your mind off the decay. But he didn't feel that warm old happy feeling of condescension in the bar that day. He hadn't felt it for a long time. All he felt now was envy. These people had expectations. Of the world, of the future, it didn't matter—expectation was such an innovative concept to him that he couldn't help but be a bit moved by what they were saying. Whatever that was.

"And the schools."

"School system going to pot. Do you know in some classes they have kids who don't speak a word—"

"—of English—"

"—the English language. Mangling it. Now, I heard how Lucky just gave a heap of money to the little elementary school here. So you can see what he's trying to attract."

"Right," he said.

"When I first heard about this conference last year, I thought, that's the middle of nowhere. But look, XMB has moved down here and I went to college with their CEO and he sings the praises. Listening to the guy, fuck. Barbecuing. Never flipped a burger in his life and he's barbecuing. Just barbecuing. Added 30 percent to his workforce and at a fraction of what it would have cost back west. Hell, I'd be barbecuing too, hours I put in."

She shook her head. "He's always at the office."

"Working those hours. XMB and Ambiex last year, but this year there's a whole new bunch coming down to check this place out. You gotta think, if it's not us, it's gonna be someone else and the plum spots'll run out. From a fiscal point of view it makes sense if you can get around the thing of picking up stakes." He slapped his palm on the table and startled everyone.

"If they want to change the name of the town to bring things up to date I say let 'em. I think Lucky's proposal is a great idea. Bottom-line-wise."

"Did you come up with the new name?" Dolly asked.

"Not me, the company I used to work for. And it's not the new name yet—it's only a proposal. There's been a little controversy in town over whether or not it's appropriate. I'm here to arbitrate, you might say."

"I think it fits. *Winthrop*—that's a bit old school, don't you think? Three martini lunches and cholesterol and all that?"

"I think it's quaint."

"Her father owns a bank. This is his kind of place. You should have seen our wedding."

"Oh Jack."

"The ice swan alone."

"Jack."

"Okay, okay. Well I think your company does good work. I think New Prospera is a great name."

He raised his mug to New Prospera. That's one vote for you.

.　.　.　.　.　.　.

When he accepted the assignment, the clients gave him a packet on the competition. Sometimes it was important to know what you were up against. Sometimes it didn't matter at all. At any rate, when asked about how he came up with the name Apex, which was often, he always kicked things off with a brief preface drawn from the information he received that fateful day.

In the promotion materials for the Johnson & Johnson Company he got the lowdown on the creation of Band-Aids. The year was 1920. The place, New Brunswick, NJ. Earle and Josephine Dickson were newlyweds. He was a cotton buyer for Johnson & Johnson, she was a housewife. He worked for the country's number-one medical supply company. She cut herself. Repeatedly. Every day it seemed. She was clumsy. She had household accidents. Through the modern lens, he told his audience (a comely young lady at a bar, poised sophisticates at a dinner party, a dentist), he interpreted the young lady's constant accidents as sublimated rebellion against the strict gender roles of her time. He'd attended a liberal-arts college. Perhaps she wanted to be a World War One flying ace, or a mechanic. He didn't know. All we have are Band-Aids, he said.

Every day Earle would come back from work to confront his wife's wounds, cotton wadding and adhesive tape in hand. He pictured her through the screen door, offering her latest domestic tragedy for his inspection when Earle came back from the office, red-eyed, anxious, what the heck, let's throw in a trembling lip. After a while, Earle decided to take himself out of the equation. He placed gauze at regular intervals onto a roll of tape, and then rolled the tape back up again. That way, whenever Josephine had one of her little cries for help, she could help herself, and if she happened to slice herself while cutting off a patch of tape, well what could be more convenient. Earle of course mentioned this innovation to his colleagues, and the rest was history and brand-name recognition, was Band-Aids, competing brands of adhesive bandages, was Apex, his toe.

. . . .

New Prospera. If he lifted the whelp by the heel he'd find the birthmark of the Fleet clan. Albert Fleet's shtick consisted of resurrecting old nomenclature motifs just before they were about to come back into vogue. Old hound dog sniffing, he had a nose for incipient revival. The good ones always came back, the steadfast prefixes, the sturdy kickers. When you counted them out, *Pro-* and *-ant* would stumble back to the top, bruised and lacerated but still standing, this month's trendy morphemes and phonemes lying at their feet in piles. Everything came around again. Languages were only so big.

He had effectively killed off *New* when New Luno hit it big, and at the time everyone warned him that it would look like he was merely chasing a trend, and that sort of thing was beneath him. Anywhere you looked that year, something was New. But success shushes those kind of accusations. If Albert was lugging New back onto the scene, you better brace yourself for a full-blown renaissance. New was new again.

Prospera, that could have come from anybody on the team. Had that romance-language armature, he was pretty sure it was a Spanish or Italian word for something. What it meant in those languages, that was unimportant, what was important was how it resonated here. The lilting *a* at the end like a rung up to wealth and affluence, take a step. A glamorous Old World cape draped over the bony shoulders of prosaic *prosperity*. Couple a cups of joe to clear the head, anybody in the firm could have come up with that one. Everyone a suspect. *Prospera* left no fingerprints on its gleaming surface.

New, new, new money, new media, new economy. New order. New Prospera. He reckoned it would look good on maps. Nestled among all those Middletons and Shadyvilles.

It wasn't that bad a name, certainly no masterpiece. When—if—he returned to work, his office would be waiting. They still needed him.

How much did he need them?

That second night in Winthrop, Old Winthrop, he went to sleep at a decent hour. He drifted off reminiscing about the tools of his trade. He drifted off thinking of kickers. Somewhere in the night he had a nightmare. Rats bubbled out of the sewers, poured out of gutters and abandoned buildings. Making little rat noises. They were everywhere, and he knew that even though they wore the skin of rats, they were in fact phonemes, bits of words with sharp teeth and tails. Latin roots, syllables to be added or subtracted to achieve an effect, kickers in their excellent variety, odd fricatives, and they chased him down. They finally cornered him in an old warehouse and he woke as they started nibbling on his vanished toe, which had reattached itself as if it had never been lost.

It was early morning. The sun was up somewhere, rebuffed by clouds. Still raining. He went to the bathroom and when he came out he noticed the envelope that had been shoved beneath the door.

The client had agreed to his conditions.

He was back to work.

TWO

. . .
. . .

HE LANDED APEX because he was at the top of his game. The bosses would call him into their office to chat, to re-assure themselves, to count the lines on his brow as they ran an idea up the flagpole. One day he stifled a burp and his pursed lips put an end to Casual Fridays. The other folks in nomencla-ture came to him with their problems, they bought him cock-tails and he offered obvious solutions to dilemmas. He wasn't exactly taxing his brain. He didn't squander names that could have been used for his projects. What he gave them were slacker names. He lent out malingerers.

He attracted clients through word of mouth. Some clients he passed off on younger, hungrier colleagues and e-mailed apologies. He was all booked up. His generosity increased his es-timation in the eyes of the lower ranks and his exclusivity won him still more clients. With the assignments he did take, he was getting faster and faster with his naming. He wasn't at the point where he could just look at something and know its name, but the answer generally came quickly and he had to sit on the name for a couple of days and pretend to ponder long and hard, or else he'd look superhuman. When he walked down the halls of the office sipping water from a paper cone, hip boots would have been a plus—he waded through a palpable morass of envy. He expected some sort of comeuppance for his efficiency. None came. In fact he was bonused repeatedly. He expected the great scales of justice to waver, for certainly his expertise was upsetting some fundamental balance in the world. There was nary a waver or a twitch. Until Apex.

His life outside of work, that was going pretty fine, too. He hadn't met that special someone but he went out a lot, made reservations at approved restaurants. Occasionally he extended a hand across the table to spark a soulful gaze. Friends of his set him up with their sisters. He had a kind of vibe he projected. Wage earning. Self-actualizing. Nice catch. A local magazine picked him as one of the City's 50 Most Eligible Bachelors. He got some mileage out of that and hit the town with new credibility. This is my face, his manner seemed to say. For the photo shoot they had him sit on a gigantic blue pill, because he had named a popular blue pill, and he wore a fine designer suit that he was not allowed to keep. The writer made a few jokes of the what-the-heck-is-a-nomenclature-consultant-you-might-ask variety. One thing about his job, he had conversation starters for sure.

His new apartment was great. There was an extra room he didn't know what to do with so after a year he got a pool table and an aquarium. He bought exotic fish for the aquarium from a specialty store. Occasionally they ate each other. There were all these fins at the bottom of the tank. Conversation starters for sure. From the balcony he could look down upon the city and think he owned it. And perhaps that feeling was in the mix when he came up with Apex. He looked down on everything. It was all so small.

. . . .

Seems like old times, he said to himself, cozying up to the desk after avoiding it for two days. "A History of the Town of Winthrop" opened with a painful crinkle. He would be prepared for his meeting that afternoon. He was a professional.

He skipped around, and after a few pages of stuff like "that famous quality of generosity that distinguishes the Winthrop family" and "Once again, the Winthrops came to the rescue in a time of need," he checked the copyright page and confirmed his suspicion. The book had been commissioned by the Winthrop Foundation. He relaxed. He'd always rather enjoyed corporate pamphlets. They did not tax his attention overmuch. You always knew how they were going to end. Winning over the town librarian for sympathetic press wasn't too much of a task, he figured. A set of leatherbound Shakespeare would do it. He wouldn't get the inside scoop, but maybe he didn't need it.

The Winthrops made their fortune in barbed wire, not too bad a gig at the end of the nineteenth century. Land grants, land grabs, you needed something cheap to keep everything in, and keep everything out. "With the zeal of a true American entrepreneur, Sterling Winthrop found customers among the region's farmers and homesteaders, who delighted in the inexpensive alternative to costly timber. Even the railroad enlisted the aid of Winthrop's fine wire to keep its lines free and clear." Innovative product, niche market, sure, sure. He jazzed his fingers on the desk excitedly. This was something he could understand. Not exactly what he was looking for, however.

Gertrude Sanders, master of the librarian arts, channeled the pioneer zeitgeist with flair, aplomb aplenty. No equivocating for Gertrude. "Where others saw untamed wilderness," she enthused, "Sterling saw endless bounty and prime opportunities." Underdeveloped land, in the modern jive: a lowly parking lot where high-rises deserved to tower. The river provided a way to move the goods. And the place was empty. Mostly. "After winning over the area's main inhabitants—a loose band of colored settlers—Winthrop opened up his factory and started producing his famous W-shaped barb, which can still be seen all over the county. Grateful for this fresh start, they passed a law and named the town Winthrop, after the man who had the courage to dream." Attracting a labor force to the town, building a community, all the usual Town-in-a-Box starter-kit stuff. Had Gertrude ever tired of the Dewey decimal thing, she would have been a shoo-in for a marketing job back East.

All that hokum. He continued to flip around. If they had created a law to change the name of the town, that meant there must have been a name to change it from. No point going to the trouble of rebranding unless there was something to rebrand. He needed to know what it was. He learned a few things, as his fingers journeyed where silverfish feared to tread. He learned about the strange mosquito plague of 1927, which ended as swiftly and mysteriously as it started, leaving none unwelted. A nearby pond was home to a very rare frog, celebrated and documented in scientific journals. A chilling woodcut confirmed the amphibian's most celebrated characteristic—an almost human gaze that could only be described as "pleading." He was about to return to the beginning when a familiar voice kicked in his adrenaline. After a single exposure, he had developed a Pavlovian response.

"Housekeeping!" She loosed her little fury against the door.

"I'm okay!"

"I need to get inside!"

"I'm okay!" he repeated. He marveled at the ridiculousness of this response, but kept his fingers crossed.

"You are preventing me from doing my job!" The two black stalks of her legs interrupted the light from beneath the door. It occurred to him that she might have an organic defect in her brain. But then she bellowed, "What are you doing that is so important!" and he decided that her problem probably claimed provenance in both nature and nurture.

He resolved to wait her out. She appeared to sense this, employing a primitive, animal awareness, growing quiet save for her quick, shallow breathing. "I will return!" she said after a time.

An hour later he was in the lobby, on the lookout for his ride. The desk clerk had called up to inform him that Mr. Winthrop would pick him up at noon. Actually, the clerk had used the word *fetch*. He saw the scenario plainly. The white-haired scion, heir to a barbed-wire empire, dispatches the limo and receives him in a smoky drawing room. That Winthrop gaze lasers in on him when he enters, but what the man is thinking exactly cannot be determined. They pose in the burgundy club chairs. Over the man's shoulder, beyond the window: the rolling estate, sprawling, undulating, alive with force. Winthrop complains about gophers, proposes solutions, and such are the tribulations of his world, eradicable by pesticide bombs. Over brandy fresh from decanters, the old dog makes his case for the Winthrop name, for tradition, for the old ways which are the best ways. His guest wears out the knees on his pants from spontaneous fits of genuflection.

So went the narrative he concocted in the lobby of the Hotel Winthrop. The job still had its paws on him. Dipping a cup into reservoirs and tasting the waters was part of the gig. If he could swallow it, the rest of the world would, too. Nomenclature consultants were supposed to have universal stomachs.

He closed his eyes, and realized the extent of his trepidation. Meeting Winthrop was no problem. He knew the type. But he was back on the job after so long, and his fingers trembled. He made them into fists in his pockets.

The desk clerk said, "Sir."

He limped out. The black Bentley crouched at the curb like a big lazy bull. A white head with little white hairs steaming off it emerged from the driver's side. "Hey, nice to meet you," the driver said. "I'm Albie." Albie wore a faded red jogging suit. Sweatbands sopped heartily at his wrists and forehead. He got the impression that Albie had just finished a few laps or had been chased by a creature. Albie said, "Hop on in."

The backseat was filled with grocery bags. A laundry-detergent spout poked out, the frilly plastic end of a bag of bread, celery stalks. "Why don't you hop up front," Albie offered, "and move a few of these things." Albie knocked a cut-up supermarket flyer off the seat, and last week's paper, and an ice scraper.

He climbed in, good leg first, and tried not to get his wet feet on the flotsam below the seat. "You can just shove that stuff under the seat," Albie said.

He shoved and settled.

"Bum leg?" Albie asked.

"Bum leg."

Albie nodded. "Been raining like this since you got here, huh? You must be bad luck or something." The man smiled. "Albie Winthrop," he said.

He shook the man's hand. Moist was the word.

They pulled out and a little dribble of coffee sloshed out of the Grande Admiral in the cup holder. Cheap plastic cup holders were not standard issue on Bentleys, he gathered, inspecting the weird little monstrosity gaffer-taped to the dashboard. Where the consumer comfort industry failed, Albie stepped in, and some time before, apparently. There were a bunch of old brown stains on the carpet. He resisted the urge to lean over and check how many miles were on the car.

Albie smiled. "Got back into town this morning," he said, "or else I'd'a come by before to meet you."

"Lucky told me you were off racing your boat somewhere?"

Albie's head bobbed. "Not my boat, no, aw," he cackled.

"Haven't had a sailboat in a long while. My old buddy Percy's boat. I'm first mate whenever he goes out. 'First mate Albie reporting for duty, capt'n!' "

"Oh," he said.

They drove a ways. The few people out on the street shuffled under slickers and umbrellas but Albie recognized them nonetheless, waving out the window excitedly and shrieking, not caring if the rain got inside. The people made their greeting motions, shook umbrellas in their direction, and trudged on. Whenever Albie passed a car, he clapped twice on the horn at the other driver and bobbed his head. "Everybody knows me," Albie explained. "I'm everybody's uncle."

The people honked back or ignored him. There's that crazy bastard again, is how he decoded these brief exchanges.

"That's old Frank's son," Albie said as a red SUV zipped toward them. Albie honked and Frank's son swerved, startled. "Frank was our foreman for many years," Albie explained. "He came up from the floor. Started on the floor with the Bessemer and moved up."

"That right?"

"Shoot. Never worked anywhere else. That's his house over there. Went there for a barbecue once. Guess you don't barbecue that much in the city, huh?"

"Hadn't noticed."

"Don't barbecue much at all, I guess." Albie honked at a

station wagon. "Hey! Mason! Hey!" And there was almost an accident.

He deliberated and then decided, yes, the Winthrop family spread qualified for estate-hood, and with a few wings to spare. They drove through an iron gate that took them past a low stone wall and wound their way up the driveway. Feral hedges clawed the car. As they approached the house he was reminded of good-for-you public television shows where there were always a lot of goings-on in the servants' quarters. But there were no more servants. No signs of life besides them in fact, until they got around back, and something crunched as the car slowed. They inspected the damage. The Mighty Wheels was now yesterday's toy, mashed to yellow-and-red bits beneath the front tire. "Aw, will you get a load of that," Albie groaned. "The tenants in the guesthouse, the kids leave all their stuff around." He shook his head.

It was always a perplexing event, he found, to help people put away their groceries. You never know where the other person's system of grocery placement connects and diverges from your own. The cabinets and drawers are avenues in a maze. One man's sponge nook is another man's soup hutch. So he leaned against the refrigerator and watched Albie unpack the week's shopping, limiting his contribution to two bag-carrying trips from the Bentley to the kitchen. He had calculated that it would require five trips to unload the car, so he exaggerated his limp to keep his trips down to a pat and optimum two.

"Have you eaten?" Albie asked, folding the last paper bag flat. "I'm going to make some hot dogs."

"Sure."

"I usually boil them, but if you want I can put them in the toaster. Put it on *broil*."

Albie interpreted his silence and prepared their repast, such as it was, placing a tiny pot of water on what had to be one of the biggest ovens he had ever seen. Albie grabbed a pair of pliers to light the burner. There were no knobs on the stove. His host offered no explanation.

"I really appreciate you coming out here all this way to help straighten out this thing," Albie said.

"It's my job."

"At first I didn't know if I could trust them to bring in someone who would give me a fair shake, you know what I mean? After what happened at the council meeting. And then you working for the company Lucky hired to think up that new name of his. How much you get paid for one of those things?"

"It varies from case to case, really. I didn't handle that account. I've been on a sabbatical."

Albie looked him over. "Heard about that," he said. "I

wasn't sure I'd be able to trust you. But then Lucky told me you were a Quincy man, and I knew I would get a fair shake. A Quincy man is a man of his word."

Albie asked him about that old groundskeeper, the one who always had a cigar plug jutting off his lips. There had been this geezer who used to trim the shrubbery and leer at the freshman girls, and he decided this must be the codger in question, so he said yes. What the hell did he know about beloved campus characters? He was not the kind who went around befriending beloved campus characters.

School days. Albie asked him what dorm he'd lived in, what year did he graduate. He didn't need to tell Albie that he'd lived next to the Winthrop Library. There was no need; Albie knew the layout of the quad and had his answer on hearing the name of the dorm. When he'd arrived at the hotel, he'd thought it was just coincidence. There were a lot of rich white people named Winthrop. But of course he of all people should have known that with names there is no coincidence. Only design, design above all. There were a lot of rich white people named Winthrop and they were all related, if not by blood then by philosophy. Old Albie's great-granddad or what have you had been a big booster of his alma mater. Their alma mater. And now that name was supposed to bind them together. Like it always did.

．　．　．　．　．　．　．　．

Some names are keys and open doors. Quincy was one.

It was the third oldest university in the country, founded on a Puritan ethic, structured on the classic British model, whatever that meant. It was prestigious. Quincy men formed the steel core of many a powerful elite, in politics, business, wherever there were dark back rooms. The sons and daughters of the famous attended Quincy and were anointed anew, for now they had two royal titles, one from the circumstance of their birth and the second from the four-year galvanizing process that occurred behind those ivy walls. The sons and daughters of the working class attended and became prows to pulverize the swells of new middle-class oceans. The presidents of foreign countries sent their sons to be educated at Quincy and they returned double agents, articulating American and Quincian directives in their native tongues. The great-grandsons of presidents would sit next to him in Modern European History and exude. Those who wanted to be president one day would leave the room when someone lit a joint. Superfamous academics and former cabinet members and Nobel laureates joined the faculty to be tenured and formaldehyded.

For the right amount of money, it was possible to get your name on a Quincy edifice. The university had a complicated

pricing plan based on square footage versus prestige of placement, from the new pool to the new dining hall to the new as-
tronomy building. Their names would live long, tattooed on the
granite skin of an eternal university. Their kids would get in, too,
no hassle. On Parents Weekend, the proud relatives swarmed the
square and snatched up sweatshirts and mugs with the bright
green Q so that everyone would know they were a satellite of
the pulsing Q star and somewhere in the Heavens, too. It was a
strong brand name, as they said in his business.

They reached out to him in his last year of high school.
He had filled out a form the previous summer at the African
American Leaders of Tomorrow conference, a weeklong program held in the nation's capital where teenagers debated U.S.
policy and tried to break curfew. The pamphlet that came in the
mail was his introduction to the world of mailing lists, target
marketing. Quincy believed in diversity. He applied. He got in,
and ended up there the next fall. What clinched it for him was
the Pre-Fresh Weekend, where they pulled out the stops to con-
vince him to come. And come he did. He got laid for the first
time at a party his freshman host had taken him to, and the
Quincy name now meant manhood, or at least the end of ex-
pectant masturbation and the start of default masturbation.

He never bought into the Quincy mystique. He did not
learn the words of the drinking songs. He did not demonize the
other colleges in their academic stratosphere. He did not come

to appreciate the peculiar magnetism of the Quincy name until he graduated, when its invisible waves sorted the world into categories, repelling the lesser alloys, attracting those of kindred ore at job interviews, parties, in bedrooms. There was no secret handshake. The two syllables sufficed. Quincy was a name that was a key, and it opened doors.

.   .   .   .

"My wife took it all," Albie moaned again. They toured the empty rooms. "Took my name and then took everything else."

He was breaking a rule, one that he didn't even know he had until he got inside Albie's place: no house calls. It was depressing. Most of the light fixtures didn't have working bulbs, so they maundered from room to room in a sullen march, their path illuminated only by the gray light from outside. Sometimes the two men were mere silhouettes, sometimes barely ghosts, and Albie's words in the air were rattling chains, it seemed to him. He grabbed items from the Hotel Winthrop and placed them on the floors and along the walls to visualize what the place had looked like a generation ago, and fire shimmied in the fireplace, and great tones erupted from the grand piano. These dim visions.

Every new door opened on emptiness, on hollowed-out history. Albie preferred the past tense. It was his new roommate, eating the last doughnut and leaving flecks of toothpaste on the bathroom mirror. "This was the game room," Albie said, as they sent dust scurrying from their steps. "This was Grandmother's room," Albie said, as a tiny square of light squeaked through an attic window.

What was there to say, he wondered, standing in the gloom, holding a paper plate. He said, "Thanks for the hot dogs."

Albie brightened instantly. "My specialty!"

They started back down the stairs. "You should rent out some rooms," he offered. Sympathy did not come easily to him, but he knew a fellow patient when he saw one. He had his misfortune, and Albie had his.

"That's what the hotel is for," Albie said. "At least I still have that." He grimaced. "We're all booked this weekend, every room. For *him*. Even when I'm making money off him for a change, he's making ten times more offa me, what Lucky'll get out of this conference in the long run."

Only the living room contained more than one piece of furniture, and they sat on the bumpy couch after Albie cleared away magazines and shooed crumbs. Mounted heads stared from one wall, the stuffed remains of the antlered and the slow-moving. Albie saw him looking at them and told him again that yes, his wife had taken everything in the divorce, everything, but he had held firm when it came to the trophies. "A man has to draw a line somewhere."

"With barbed wire," he said. He pointed above the fireplace, where a thick braid of metal was mounted on dark wood. Not a trophy but a monument.

"Barbed wire! *Drawing a line*, exactly! I knew I could talk to you," Albie exclaimed gleefully. He skipped over to the mantel and ran a finger along the metal. "This was our barb," he cooed, tracing the butterfly-shaped loop. "Mark of distinction. Every wire manufacturer had their own barb, so you knew what you were buying. People go to buy a new bundle, they'd look at this W right here and know they were buying quality."

"Your brand."

"All over the plains, they buy Winthrop Wire, they buy quality. They knew this. Nobody knows about this stuff anymore except people here. And soon . . ." His hand fell.

Albie returned to the couch, frowned, and recounted the whole sad story of The Day of the Doublecross. He didn't know why it had happened, but Regina and Lucky had "bushwacked" him. For the life of him, he didn't understand. Lucky Aberdeen—why, Albie had embraced the man like a brother, despite all that had gone on between them real estate–wise. And Regina, they were practically blood relations— their families went so far back it was practically historical.

The day of the vote, Albie had just finished visiting old Marcia Newton, who had broken her hip and was bedridden. (He recalled the days after his misfortune, when he was bedridden and unable to escape. It was people like Albie who had made him barricade himself in his apartment during his convalescence.) Albie was in fine spirits when he walked into the meeting, full of his good deed, and ready to discuss the new SLOW CHILDREN signs. The controversy over whether to put up two or four signs had been simmering for weeks, and that day the city council would settle the matter once and for all. Just the three of them at the table, the way it had always been for generations. The city council, the old, benevolent tribunal. Majority rules.

And then Lucky said that they had another matter to settle before they could proceed to the matter of Slow Children: the name of the town. There's been a lot of talk in town, Lucky told him, about whether or not Winthrop as a name reflects new market realities, the changing face of the community. (As Albie's mouth formed the words *market realities*, his lips arched toward his nostrils and his eyes slitted, so sour were the syllables.) Talk, what talk, Albie asked, he hadn't heard any talk and he was practically the heart of the town. Lucky appeared not to hear him. Lucky kept on with his nonsense. "In that idiotic vest." Lucky said: It's been proposed that maybe we should look back to the town charter of Winthrop and invoke the laws that define this town. That maybe we, the city council, should run the numbers and take a vote on whether to change the name of Winthrop to something more appropriate.

"You can imagine what I was feeling," Albie complained, putting two fingers to his lips and belching. "I tried to get them to talk to me, but they were like stone. I said, 'How could you do this to me, I'm your good old pal.' Bringing up that old law. It hadn't been used since they changed the name to Winthrop in the first place. Was it still on the books, I wanted to know, but they weren't having it. Wouldn't listen to me. And I tell you, I thought it was a done deal once they won the vote, two to one. I was thinking, how long have they been planning this? Voting to change the name. Digging up some old law no one ever thought to take off the books. Putting one over on Uncle Albie. 'You don't do that to your uncle,' I said. 'I'm everybody's uncle!' I turned to Regina and told her, 'Regina, look me in the eyes.' But she wouldn't look at me. And Lucky went, 'Now that that's decided, let's move on to the matter of the new name itself.' He brought out that stupid suggestion of his—New Prospera—and went, 'All in favor, say aye.' But then Regina double-crossed him, and boy, oh boy, was he surprised! You should have seen his face," Albie said, his voice cracking. "We sat there deadlocked. Every name—mine, Lucky's, Regina's—had one vote, and no one would budge. It was the three of us, and no one would budge."

Albie looked exhausted.

"This law was put on the books to change the name of the town to Winthrop."

"It was only a settlement really," Albie said, "where Regina's family decided to stop one day. There wasn't any thought to it. They just dropped their bags here."

"But what was it called?"

"Oh. They called it Freedom."

Freedom, Freedom, Freedom. It made his brain hurt. Must have been a bitch to travel all that way only to realize that they forgot to pack the subtlety.

. . . .

Apex was manufactured by Ogilvy and Myrtle. They got their start in 1896 as commercial suppliers of sterile gauzes and medicinal plasters. From what he could tell, theirs was a small but sturdy outfit with solid distribution in the south, catering mostly to hospitals. He imagined Ogilvy and Myrtle Sterile Bandages being applied to the hip wounds of the day. Got kicked in the head by a horse, fell off a stagecoach, you knew where to go.

Things picked up during World War One, when they put in a successful bid for a military contract. An assured client base of patriotic casualties enabled them to enter the age of mass production. Blood in their business was down-payment money and lines of credit. A couple of years later, once Johnson & Johnson unleashed the noble Band-Aid, O and M joined the adhesive-bandage revolution with gusto.

Any way you looked at it, Ogilvy and Myrtle's Sterile Bandages were shoddy pieces of work. It must have been those military contracts, he speculated—government money will lull the best of souls into short-shrifting, he'd seen it happen. Whatever the reason, poor craftsmanship was the star the company ship steered by, and they tacked expertly. Number one, he observed, the rectangle of folded cotton absorbed nothing, and immediately after application brown blotches soaked through. Might as well walk around with a spouting artery if that's going to happen. And the not-Band-Aids had a temperament. The moment he put one on, it was overcome with an unbearable self-loathing and the edges rolled up on themselves, too shy for this world. Whereupon it was only a few seconds before the gummy sides were clotted with dirt and they were even more abject. In showers, they went AWOL first thing, abetted by the particularly water-soluble adhesive, leaping from skin for the safety of the drain. Afterward when you should have been drying, you had to root around amid the hair and suds down there to prevent clogging. Water or no water, they self-destructed after twelve hours regardless, so that when you reached into your pocket for your wallet, the bandage clung to the rim of the pocket and tore off, the pocket pulled the scab off, and you bled on your clothes and dollars. A person couldn't win with those things.

In the fifties, they relaunched their brand as Dr. Chickie's Adhesive Strips, hoping that a homey image might rustle up a little market share. These were the days before the advent of nomenclature firms, the Dark Ages. To people like him, the amateur namers of yore were like medieval doctors who never saw a patient unless armed with a bucket of leeches. Perhaps in its historical context, removed from modern cynicism, Dr. Chickie might have been a figure of apparent trust and authority, staring back at the wounded from the front of the tin box. He wore a white smock, lascivious grin bulging behind a white mask, and he peered through deep goggles that would not have been out of place on a World War Two flying ace. To his eyes, Dr. Chickie came off like a pediatrician who kept a box of special pictures in his desk drawer, the kind you had to send away to Amsterdam to get developed.

Dr. Chickie prescribed no special remedy for the unpopularity of O and M's adhesive strips. The good doctor ministered to the same handful of loyal patients for years, doddering on until the overhaul that cued him onto the stage. When he got the assignment, the only mental association he had with Dr. Chickie was deranged relatives. When he went to visit his deranged relatives they always had rusting tins of Dr. Chickie in their medicine cabinets. O and M had stopped packaging their strips in metal tins only a few years earlier, as if the plastic and cardboard revolutions had never happened. Market research bore out his impressions. The only people who used the product lived in small hamlets where everybody believed Truman was still the president; on visiting their homesteads the mailman shoved in pitches for land deals in Florida and sweepstakes guarantees and little else. Mummies that they were, they didn't need Dr. Chickie's Adhesive Strips anyway. What was there to sop? What they needed were brooms, to sweep up the dust that fell out of the nicks in their bodies. These people were not the kind you tried to seduce through advertisements in tony magazines. Only the rise of managed health care kept the company in the black. The military, HMOs: O and M had a facility for finding those in need of bargains bought in bulk. Nonetheless, they wanted a leg up in the domestic field.

It was quite a situation.

Really, what else were they going to do?

They came to him and he saved them.

. . . .

No, Albie's wife hadn't taken everything in the divorce. She had left him his inappropriate emotional reactions to small things. Before they got back into the Bentley, Albie noticed the crushed toy in the driveway and murmured, "It's a damn shame," shaking his head as if rendering verdict on the entirety of cruel nature. A frankfurter made him smile, a broken toy sullen. He hoped that Albie's melancholy might put an end to conversation for a time, but Winthrop Lane had other plans. It must be unfortunate to be so unsettled at the sight of your name. Particularly when your name was everywhere.

"This is the first road they put in," Albie told him, "so that they could get supplies back and forth. Keep following it and you'll hit the factory. Before that it was just woods. Maybe there were some Indians or something, but they didn't have a road." Albie winced. "Probably want to change the name of the road, too. It's like they want to erase it all."

"I don't do roads."

"It's simple tradition. You know what it means to be a Quincy man—we're all brothers. It doesn't matter where you come from, once you walk into those ivy halls, you're in the brotherhood. Women, too, now that they let women in. They got a right. I tell you, I go back to visit and I can't help but say, Golly, look at how it's changed! You got all kinds of people, from all over the world. Handicap access, so they can wheel up there, it's great. But even in my day, there was that spirit. A community of like-minded people. Had a black fella lived in my dorm. There were only five or six, but you have to understand the times. Good fella, quiet. Milton, I think that was his name. Lived downstairs. Liked to swim, if I remember correctly."

"Wow." He had found, in his life, that it was always a good

policy to flee when white people felt compelled to inform you about their black friend, or black acquaintance, or black person they saw on the street that morning. There were many reasons to flee, but in this case the pertinent one was that the reference was intended to signal growing camaraderie. He recognized landmarks on the road, and realized that they were almost at the hotel.

"Quincy days—they were good times, right? They mean something." His eyes sparkled. "There is a bond. It's the same thing here, that's what I'm telling you—look! There's old Gil and his little rug rats. Hey Gil! What was I—okay, okay, Winthrop *means* something. Goode's people, sure, they're the ones first settled here, sure. Can't dispute that even if I wanted to, it's a historical fact. But it was nothing 'til my great-great-granddad opened up the factory here. Just a bunch of trees until there was a Winthrop name to say: This is here. It's tradition. Guys like you and me, we understand that."

At the curb outside the hotel, a white shuttle bus disgorged passengers. Recruits fresh from the airport, dressed in the uniform of their kind, primary-color polo shirts and khakis. Albie pulled up and grimaced. "Will you get a load of that," he muttered. "Marching in like a bunch of ducks. Ain't that a kick in the pants—only time this place makes any money is when Lucky has one of his things going on."

He slid out of the passenger seat and said to Albie, "Can't

stop progress," without thinking. It was a catchall phrase of his, something to put out there when he felt too indifferent to come up with a more engaged response. He instantly regretted his mistake. He looked back into the car. There sat Albie, pooled in the front seat: privilege gone soft in its own juices.

"No, you can't stop progress, can you?" Albie sighed. Did his eyes glisten, or was it a trick of the light? "Listen," Albie said, "I know you have responsibilities. You got your job. But you're here to be objective, right? You can see what they're trying to do, can't you? They're trying to take away something that means something."

They left it at that.

He found himself walking automatically to the hotel bar and stopped. He considered the situation, and then permitted his subconscious to have its way. He had only been away for a few hours, but there was no reason his afternoon could not be categorized as a hard day's work.

The joint was packed. He shuffled through. You could have called it Happy Hour, had Muttonchops not been glowering behind the bar. The bartender poured him a beer as soon as he sat down on the single empty barstool. He pictured the shuttle buses, one by one, as they navigated the twisty roads from the big city, full of Lucky's recruits, buckled up and secure. The visitors dispersed once they hit the elevator, but only briefly. They washed their faces and flossed and then they made their way down here.

Freedom. He whistled. If he'd offered up Freedom in a meeting, he'd have been run out of town, his colleagues in full jibber behind him, waving torches. It was like something from the B-GON days, an artifact of the most pained and witless nomenclature. Roach B-GON, Rat B-GON. Hope B-GON. Freedom was so defiantly unimaginative as to approach a kind of moral weakness.

He didn't hear the punch line. Only the laughter. Like everyone else at the bar, he turned to find the source of the racket, and there was Lucky, in the back of the room, in his Indian Vest, surrounded by his weekend guests. Lucky was in raconteur mode, he could tell by the job-well-done smirk on the man's face. The laughter continued as one man initiated another round of braying; no one wanted to be the first to stop. They were a pretty mixed group, Lucky's future business partners and incipient flunkies—put a picture of Sterling Winthrop's laborers next to a picture of Lucky's multiculti crew and caption the tableau CHANGING TIMES. Jack Cameron, the man he'd met last night, hadn't been a representative sample. The crowd in the corner could have been an Apex ad, to tell you the truth, so well-hued were they.

Lucky spotted him at the bar and winked and started over.

The Help Tourists stepped aside, each one attempting to catch Lucky's eye. This was how people reacted when you had the touch. It was how he'd pictured Albie Winthrop on his walks through town, before he'd met the man. Not that diminished thing whose empty kingdom he had just departed. He despised himself his earlier generosity toward Albie. Be a man, for Christ's sake, he should have told him. Not indulged his weakness.

"Hello, friend!" Lucky said. "I can tell from your face that you met with our favorite son."

"You're right."

"You need a drink, then," Lucky opined, and invited him to join their table. Without instruction, Muttonchops placed six cans of Brio on a platter, which Lucky carried to the back of the room. Man of the people. He followed. As the two men jostled their way through, the assembled surreptitiously checked him out, trying to gauge his importance, and what was with the limp. Lucky dispensed the cans of Brio and introduced him with a chipper "This is the man who's going to put our little town on the map—literally!"

He endured the usual round of questions about the nature of his profession before the subject turned to the new wireless standard. Apparently the new wireless standard was quite precocious. He kept silent. He took notice of his placement in the group. The words *cordoned off* occurred to him. Although the eight of them were gathered in a perfect circle—broken only now and then by someone leaning over the table to pick up a Brio—he felt exiled, a physical disengagement. This was not mere disinterest made into a palpable thing; Lucky possessed a zone of power. The computer entrepreneur and his Help Tourists were separated from him by invisible barbed wire that maintained a border. There is within, and there is without.

"It was such a quick ride down from the airport," observed a young Latino woman. CFO of some fledgling e-commerce outfit. Router of arcane information. Repetitive stress injury candidate, fiddling with the levers on her office chair. She said, "I didn't realize we were so close."

Lucky smiled. "No traffic, you can make it in an hour. Some people even commute from the city. We don't recommend it, but it's an option." He took a sip of Brio. "I know some of you are worried that you'll miss all that a big city has to offer. It's a huge fucking thing to move out here, I know that. It's a big idea, but if you were afraid of big ideas, I wouldn't have asked you here."

He noticed that he was the only one drinking beer. Follow the leader. He wondered exactly what percentage of life came down to good marketing skills. He settled on 90 percent. The other ten was an antacid, to help settle things.

Lucky said, "Gimme 2.0, my friends, give me 2.0. One thing you're going to learn this weekend is that I'm always looking for Version 2.0. One of our teams finishes a project—they've been busting their asses day and night—they finish it, show it to me, and what do I say? 'Good job—but what's Version 2.0?' Because whatever it is, it's not good enough. You can always tweak it, there are always ways to make it better. So I say: I love this town, but what's the next thing? Where's 2.0? I'll tell you. *You're* 2.0, *we're* 2.0, my friend the consultant standing right here, looking like the Sphinx come to town, *he's* 2.0." Lucky squinted at him. "What do you think of that, friend?"

He said, "Hmm."

Lucky slapped him on the back and turned to his audience. "He's working! He's taking it all in! That's the burden of genius! Wouldn't have it any other way." Lucky looked at the can in his hand. "God, I love this stuff!"

Somebody said, "I've never had it before, but it's really good!" and the rest of them agreed heartily.

He quickly finished off his beer and limped upstairs. When he got back safely to his room, he stepped on the note that had been slipped under the door. It was written in a maniac scrawl, what happened when the right-handed switch it up and use their left. It read, "I have honored your request for PRIVACY but will admit to ownership of a rising anger at your refusal to allow ME entrance. This HEAVY FEELING sits on my chest. WHO do you think you are?"

He looked around. His mess was as it had been. Nothing had been touched.

.   .   .   .

The number-six adhesive bandage in the country wanted to re-create itself as the number-two adhesive bandage in the country. There was no use trying to overtake Band-Aid, the number-one adhesive bandage. Band-Aid had recognition and fidelity across generations and generations. Generations and generations of accidents and the scars to remind people of what Band-Aids had helped them through. The name was the thing itself, and that was Holy Grail territory. But you could try to catch up with that, become number two, by claiming a certain percentage of future accidents as your own. So men schemed.

Enter the whiz kid consultant. "Not me," he always joked when he told the tale, "although I'm flattered, really. I'm referring to the hypothetical bespectacled whiz kid who thought up multicultural adhesive bandages." Said whiz kid was another of his kind, a lonesome operative doing the same work, believing and disbelieving the same half-assed philosophies. He pictured him strutting down the aisles of drugstores, hands clasped behind his back, surveying the latest advances in adhesive-bandage technology, factotum trailing. The clear strip. The happily colored adhesive strips for children, with their little stars and turtles and crescent moons. The waterproof wonders and the antibiotic-soaked specials. The adhesive bandage had come of age while O and M was still trying to save a few cents on sub-standard gum formulas. The drugstores had ample shelf space, there was always more room for adhesive-bandage innovation. The antifungal sprays could be displaced to a niche in Aisle 6. This consultant, his opposite number and brother, he wished he knew his name, told his clients that what they needed was a hook.

And here he tried to re-create the consultant's pitch for his listeners. The man walked around the conference room table, provoking the good men in their good suits to reconsider the basic laws of their profession. Band-Aids are flesh-colored, the man said. Most adhesive bandages are flesh-colored. Are advertised as such. And it did not occur to anyone to ask, whose flesh is this? It ain't mine, and with that the man pulls back one sleeve to reveal his wrist, and the skin there.

The whiz kid said, You manufacture this thing and call it flesh. It belongs to another race. I have different ideas about what color flesh is, he told them. We come in colors. We come in many colors. And we want to see ourselves when we look down at ourselves, our arms and legs. Around the table the men listened, and soon afterward they got to work. Somebody give this guy a raise.

At Ogilvy and Myrtle they knew the neighborhoods,

some block by block, and they knew the hues of the people who lived there. They knew the cities and the colors of their mayors. They knew the colors of clientele and zip codes and could ship boxes accordingly.

They devised thirty hues originally, later knocked them down to twenty after research determined a zone of comfort. It didn't have to be perfect, just not too insulting. What they wanted was not perfect camouflage but something that would not add insult to injury. In the modern style, the gentlemen of Ogilvy and Myrtle learned to worship databases, and linked fingers before altars of data. There was a large population of Norwegian Americans in the Midwest; O and M sent them a certain shipment. And there was a denomination of Mexican Americans in the Southwest; O and M sent them a certain shipment. The cities and hamlets had hues. The shipments were keyed, bands of colors were strategically bundled together. Given their particular business history, O and M possessed long-standing supply networks to poor countries—their cruddy craftsmanship demanded this—and to these poor countries they shipped appropriate boxes to their inevitably brown-skinned populations. The school nurses of integrated elementaries could order special jumbo variety packs, crayon boxes of the melanin spectrum, to serve diversity.

Even he had to admire the wonder of it all. The great rainbow of our skins. It was a terrain so far uncharted. Pith helmets necessary. The fashioners of clear adhesive strips almost recognized this but didn't take the idea far enough. The world of the clear strip was raceless; it did not take into account that we sought ourselves, like sought like, that a white square of white cotton wadding attached to transparent tape dispelled the very illusion they attempted to create. Criminy—an alien square of white on the skin, well that was outside the pale of even the albinoest albino. The deep psychic wounds of history and the more recent gashes ripped by the present, all of these could be covered by this wonderful, unnamed multicultural adhesive bandage. It erased. Huzzah.

When the consultant looked down at his arm, what did he see? Was the man his color, something else, was he *flesh*-colored? When the man looked down at his arm, did he observe business opportunities, an unexploited niche, an overlooked market, or something else? The man saw the same thing he saw. The job.

. . . .

Friday morning he stood before the plywood fence, looking at the COMING SOON OUTFIT OUTLET sign. Head cocked, dumb gaze, stalled mid-step: any observer would have translated his body language into the universal pose of *lost*. Reception's directions had led him to this spot. He looked up and down the street, but didn't see where he could have made the mistake.

A door in the fence scraped inward, revealing a scruffy young white dude whose wrecked posture, rumpled clothes, and shallow expression marked a life of few prospects, and fewer misgivings about the lack of said prospects. An existence lived in the safety and hospitality of that protected nature preserve called the American Middle Class. The name Skip was embroidered over the left breast of his striped mechanic's shirt, which meant in all probability his name was not Skip. Not Skip awkwardly steered a dolly onto the sidewalk, grunting.

He informed Not Skip that he was looking for the library.

The dude set the dolly level, his hand anxiously frisking the stack of boxes to ensure they did not tumble, and jerked his head toward the door. "They're closed," he mumbled. "But you can see for yourself if you don't believe me."

Not Skip struggled past him and he glanced up at the Latin phrase engraved above the Winthrop Library's doorway. That was going to have to go, unless it was Latin for Try Our New Stirrup Pants. Probably not the first time one of his clients had displaced a library, and probably not the last.

On the rare occasions that he entered libraries, he always felt assured of his virtue. If they figured out how to distill essence of library into a convenient delivery system—a piece of gum or a gelcap, for example—he would consume it eagerly, relieved to be finished with more taxing methods of virtue gratification. Helping little old ladies across the street. Giving tourists directions. Libraries. Alas there would be no warm feeling of satisfaction today. The place was a husk. The books were gone. Where he would usually be intimidated by an army of daunting spines, there were only dust-ball rinds and Dewey decimal grave markers. As if by consensus, all the educational posters and maps had cast out their top right-hand corner tacks, so that their undersides bowed over like blades of grass. Nothing would be referenced this afternoon, save indomitable market forces.

Even the globe was gone. Over there on a table in the corner he saw the stand, the bronze pincers that once held the world in place, but the world was gone. Next to the stand he spied a small messy pile of books with colorful spines, which he momentarily mistook for a pile of This Month's Sweaters, mussed by grubby consumers and waiting for the soothing, loving ministrations of the salesgirl.

"We're not open," she said. "Middle of next week we'll be open around the corner." She rounded a bank of desolate shelves, this young white chick with dyed black hair, the twenty or forty bracelets on her wrists jangling like the keys of a prison guard. Salesgirl or librarian? She dropped a load of children's books on a desk, and wheezed loudly, out of proportion to her burden. Her clothes were dull gray where the light hit them, the faded favorite gray of jet-black clothes washed too many times. He didn't peg her as homegrown talent, and she made an unlikely librarian, stereotype-wise. Nonetheless, he decided: One bracelet for every shush.

"Oh," he said.

"Come back next week for all your shopping needs," she said. "If you need to use the Web, you're welcome to," she added, brushing dust off her skirt. "They want us to keep 'em on until we have to turn 'em off." Along the back wall there was a line of six computers, their cursors blinking impatiently. A pyramid of books anchored one side of the computer table, with one copy face-out on top in the apex, and he recognized the cover of Lucky Aberdeen's autobiography, *Lucky Break: How a Small-Town Boy Took On Corporate America—and Won!* Above the computers, the bowed-over corner of a promotional poster obscured the final few words of Lucky's motto, which, conveniently, was also the publicity tagline: DREAMING IS A CINCH WHEN YOU—

He asked if there were digital archives on the town's history, which did not strike him as a funny question, certainly not worthy of a smirk. "No one's ever asked that question before," she told him, "not ever. All the stuff we have is in good old-fashioned books. And it's in boxes. You have to come back next week." Perhaps his face revealed something, although when he reviewed the encounter later, he felt confident that he had not slipped. It was ridiculous to think that he had registered disappointment over something as unimportant as a job. More likely, her librarian instincts had awakened after days of packing things up. She asked, "Is there something in particular you're looking for?"

"I wanted to find anything about the law on changing the name of the town."

She made the connection and her face brightened. "You're that outside consultant, right? I heard about you." He'd never heard someone say that particular c word with such relish. "What do you want to know?" she offered. "I'm the one who did all the legwork on that for Lucky." She straightened, and if she wore glasses she would have slid them up her nose. "Who else are you going to ask but the town librarian?"

"Some general background on the switch to Winthrop from Freedom," he said.

"It happened in this very room," she said, suddenly center stage on the set of a public television documentary. "This was the town hall before it was the library. There were three people on the city council—Goode and Field, the two black guys who first settled here, and Sterling Winthrop, he of the barbed-wire fortune. Have you met Albie, yet?"

"He's everybody's uncle."

She snorted. "It was basically a business deal, really," she said. "The Light and the Dark had claim to the land. There—"

He interrupted her. "What was that Light?"

"The Light and the Dark were Goode's and Field's nicknames," she explained. "Goode was the sunny-disposition guy and Field was the grumpy one. Like the Odd Couple. So that's how they got their nicknames."

The Light, the Dark. Freedom. My people, my people. Regina's forebears were the laziest namers he'd ever come across. He grimaced and asked her to continue with her story.

The librarian told him that there were a lot of black towns in the state at that point in time. "If everything wasn't packed up, I could show you some really interesting stuff about the all-black towns around here," she lamented. "Winthrop comes along and falls in love with the area—that river traffic, at any rate—and so they decided to make it all legal. I think it was hard to argue with the kind of access Winthrop'd provide to the outside world—having a white guy up front—so they got together to incorporate the town. Drew up a town charter, elected themselves the town council, and got all their ducks in a row."

"Might as well go with the devil you know."

"He wasn't going to hassle them or lynch them or burn them out or whatever, and at that point you needed a certain number of citizens in order to incorporate and be officially recognized by the state. There was a whole community already here to pump up the numbers. Both sides got something out of it."

"So why the law, then?" he asked. "Why not go change the name outright? They were the village elders." The question had been bothering him, and the previous night before going to sleep, he'd hit the books to answer it. While he'd learned plenty about barbed wire, and smelting patents, and the long-range vision of a certain entrepreneur, all he'd found of his quarry were suspicious don't-look-too-close constructions. *They decided to change the name. The name was changed.* Wording and phrasing familiar as the essential grammar of modern business.

"I think the people liked the name Freedom," she said, shrugging. "It sounds corny, but it meant something to them. A couple of years earlier, they'd been slaves. Now they had rights, they were official. They liked being citizens, and citizens have a government with rules and whatnot. The way I interpreted it is, Goode and Field wanted to do it right. Do it by the book. Made it a law, made it legal, and then voted to change the name."

Something sounded off to him, but he didn't pursue it. He heard Not Skip bang his way through the door. The librarian gave the kid a look and he rolled his way out of sight. "We're going to be here all weekend at this rate," she complained.

"What do you think of this name-change business?" he asked.

"Now or back then?"

"Now, Lucky's thing."

She shrugged, halfheartedly this time, her pure apathy undermining the very expression of apathy. *Slimpies*: Ready-to-Wear Shrugs for When You Just Don't Have It in You. "He's the boss man," she drawled. It turned out Lucky had lured her to Winthrop a few years ago. There had been a file-sharing program Lucky was very keen on, and she was part of a team brought in to dig around in the kernel and try to figure out how it worked.

"Rip it off."

"Sure. And we worked for a few weeks, and then Lucky informed the team that he'd bought the company outright. I had just moved down, and I didn't want to go back, so I took this job." She pursed her lips. "You can't blame Lucky for being Lucky," she said evenly. "It's like blaming water for being wet. This job's not so bad. Mostly I tell people how to use the browsers and make sure the kids aren't looking for porn. When Lucky asked me to do a little background on the olden days, I was pretty happy to have something to do. 'Can I get some intel on this name thing?' " she said, imitating him. "That doesn't mean I'm all up in his Kool-Aid, if you know what I mean."

"Yup."

She sighed, her eyes drifting to the empty stacks, and she was reminded of her task. "Anything else?" she asked.

Something in her movements jostled a heavy-lidded thing in his brain stem, and he had a very concrete image of the librarian in her bedroom, on her bed, leaning back, bit of thigh, little feather of panties just visible. He realized it was his first sexual thought in months, not counting what had been wrought by that damned series of shampoo commercials. The shampoo commercial as arena for erotic play had alternately vexed and titillated him during his convalescence.

She said, "Hey," and he said, "Sorry?"

"I said, the old archives are in the new building already, but if I come across the box, I'll let you know. If you want to look for yourself."

He thanked her and wished her good luck.

As he reached the door, she yelled after him. "You should try a cane. Canes are cool."

He looked back and gave her a brief nod. "Maybe I will," he said, even though he'd already done the cane thing, months ago. It didn't take.

.   .   .   .

It was easy. Apex.

He had been saving Apex for a while. It had come to him in a dream that everything was Apex.

Of course the summit, human achievement, the best of civilization, and of course something you could tumble off of, fall fast.

Was: waterproof, flexible, multicultural, recommended by four out of five doctors in a highly selective survey.

Apex was a name you could rely on.

The little part on the top of the pyramid, tons of stone dragged across the sand to make this thing. The eye on the top of the pyramid as it appears on the dollar bill. He had heard this was a symbol of immense power according to mystics. What the mystics saw was Apex. It was the currency of the world.

In its natural state, it possessed one of the great product kickers of our time. The holy *ex*. A classic.

Take it for a spin—it was good to go.

We try to give you a glimpse of your unattainable selves. Keeps you docile.

And when their skin was cut by roses or knives or lovers' words they reached for Apex.

That great grand plosive second syllable. Quite the motherfucker, that.

Not too bad for chanting, either, he thought. Repeated to fascistic crescendo, on flags around the square, streaming from streetlamps and across the backs of horses and flapping from the top of the elegant plaza in benign intensity.

The clients came to the office, genuflecting, this or that object on its velvet bed, polished of human fingerprints in the cab on the way to the meeting. None of those things deserved Apex so he kept the name tight, looking over his shoulder as he spun the combination to the safe to make sure it was still where he kept it. No one knew of his treasure and he thought: One day.

Didn't history rise to a point? Couldn't they look down from today and survey all that had come before, all that little stuff we squinted at that was not special and so far away, and pronounce ourselves Apex?

He saw the first ads for Apex. They said Apex Hides the Hurt, and he said, of course it does.

.　.　.　.　.　.　.　.

On his return from the library, he had to squeeze past all the pretty shuttle buses queued up in front of the hotel. They idled, hummed, and almost curtsied, it seemed to him. He sighed. Some people went in for *driftwood*, others were suckers for *cellar door*, but as far as commonplace word units went, he had always been rather fond of *shuttle bus*, and back in his office days had spent many an afternoon advocating its case.

The sound of everyday things was a constant topic, with regard to what they might occasionally chisel off the mundane, but that was just pretext for him. Say it five times fast, he maintained—shuttle bus shuttle bus sounded like leaves whispering to each other in your textbook primordial glen. Never mind the initial mental image of the ungainly vehicle, and its battle between intimacy and utility—a shuttle bus approaches grace on the asphalt of humility, he insisted. Inevitably, his colleagues shook their heads when he got to that part, but he never wavered. As perfect containers of that moment between anticipation and event, as roving four-wheeled or six-wheeled conveyances of hope, shuttle buses cannot be blamed if the destination disappoints, if desire is counterfeited, if after all that dreaming all we have to show are ashes. Shuttle buses, at worst, were unwitting accomplices. Being a shuttle bus, he argued, meant never having to say you were sorry. He always expected applause when he finished.

So he felt nostalgic about the old days for a minute there, as he watched Lucky's pilgrims vibrate before the little shuttle buses. They parsed the signs taped below the bubble windows, searching for the names of their chosen diversions: THE GOLFING EXPERIENCE, BUBBLING BROOK SPA AND MENTAL

RELAXATION CLINIC, AU NATUREL. He wondered how many miles away these places were, how far into the region Lucky had reached in order to pull these people to his breast. Every half-baked amusement for fifty miles around had probably been conscripted to his purpose. He had half a notion to slip on board one of these chariots—Thinkin' 'Bout Spelunkin' or Take a Hike—and lose himself with the others.

Instead, he took a seat on one of the uncomfortable red sofas in the lobby. The housekeeper needed more time. His trip to the library had been shorter than he'd calculated, and he didn't want to risk another encounter with She of the Rolling Doom. Better give it twenty minutes, he decided, and he felt a knot or two beneath his shoulder blades ease. It was nice to have a nemesis—on that point there could be no disagreement—but this feeling went beyond the usual joy of combat with a mortal enemy, of having a constant companion through gripe and grudge. The housekeeper was turning out to be a convenient lightning rod, drawing off excess hostility and resentment. He couldn't take it out on his clients; that would be unprofessional. Masterstroke here was to use her as she was using him: as scapegoat and punching bag for unruly stuff best undirected, for now, at the true targets. He took a deep breath, heard a voice from his single yoga class years ago and held that breath, stretching his arms luxuriously. *Shuttle bus, shuttle bus*, he whispered. Ah, forget the spa, forget the oatmeal soaps and obscure incenses. He was better already.

Taken with the novelty of this feeling of well-being, he didn't notice the little white man standing over him until the flash blinded him. He was thoroughly startled, his arms and legs jerking ridiculously. His perimeter of personal space had expanded in the months since his misfortune, and this specimen, with his nefarious digital camera, had crossed the line so quickly and efficiently that he cursed himself for such a grave security lapse. Later that afternoon, when he considered the border of his personal space, he reckoned that it was not so much a perfect circle, as commonly thought, but an irregular blob shape, jellyfishy hither and yon, and constantly shifting.

"I was told you might be available for an interview?" the man said, depositing the camera in a pocket and withdrawing his card in one agile movement. He had the pale, narrowed features of some burrowing creature, a scraper of soil, no close friend of daylight. The tiny eyeglasses civilized him, promoting him to a talking burrowing creature of children's books, an officious supporting player, Sir Gary Groundhog or Postulating Possum. His name in fact was Jurgen Cross, and the card contained a phone number and an e-mail address, but no other specifics. "I'm writing a feature about Aberdeen and Lucky for the *Daily Register*," Jurgen chirped, "and was told you might offer up a few words?"

"Who told you that?"

Jurgen fell down into the couch next to him. "It will only take a moment—thank you so much!" It was hard to account for his peculiar brand of joy. "What do you think of Winthrop?" Jurgen inquired, grinning.

"It's nice."

"Why is a good name so important? A name is the first thing outsiders hear of a place, yes? It's the face that we show the world."

"That's true."

"Aberdeen Software is the biggest thing to happen to the town since the barbed-wire factory."

"Is that a question?"

"I'm writing the article in my head as we speak."

"Is that why you're not taking any notes or using a tape recorder?" he asked. The back of his neck felt hot, and he looked around for someone to blame or someone to lean on, but of course there was no one in either category, only Help Tourists with gym bags in one hand and sunblock in the other.

Jurgen tapped his temple and smiled. "I've got it all up here, trust me. What makes New Prospera such a great name? It's very modern, isn't it?"

"If you compare the two names," he began, and then looked around the lobby. Anyone overhearing this conversation would think him an idiot. Across the room, two Help Tourists interrogated a map, tapping it in places with their fingers. Their downcast heads presented to him the nearly identical bald circles on their skulls. The freckles were in different places, though. He said, "It's not my area of expertise, but Winthrop is a traditional place-name, insisting on the specific history of the area and locating it in one man. The man embodies an idea, and the name becomes the idea. Standard stuff. New Prospera is what you might call the contemporary approach. Break it down into parts, and each part is referring to a quality that they want to attach to the town. They bring the external in, import it you might say, to this region."

"Import it you might say."

"Right. Winthrop is a mystery to outsiders. Who was Winthrop, what did he do? You have to come here to find out. Why should I care, make me care—this is what outsiders think. But New Prospera, you start making up all sorts of stuff the moment you hear it. It has associations and images. Coming here confirms or disappoints the scenarios in your head."

"Scenarios in your head."

"Sure. But there are actually three names we're talking about here. If you consider Freedom—"

"Your company came up with the name New Prospera. What makes your firm the preeminent identity firm in the country? The tops?"

"I actually don't work for them anymore," he said, raising his hands as if to wave off misconception. "I didn't—"

"What I find so interesting is the world of opportunities that a wonderful name like New Prospera will bring to the town," Jurgen said. "Big businesses looking for a tax-friendly haven, young people who want a fresh start. To start a family in a positive environment close to the conveniences of a big city."

The moment stretched. Then he said, "Huh?"

"Are you keeping it real?"

"Sorry?"

"Are you keeping it real?"

"What?"

"Are you keeping it real?"

"What?"

"Are you keeping it real?"

"Yes."

Jurgen squinted off into the distance. "I think that's about all I have. Is there any question I haven't asked that you'd like to be asked, and then talk naturally about?"

"No."

"What's your favorite color?"

"Blue."

"Let's say green." Jurgen stood up quickly and extended his hand. "Thank your so much for your time. You've been really helpful and this was very refreshing." And with that the reporter scurried out of the lobby to forage for the winter.

The man had been sent by Lucky, to soften him up for their meeting the next afternoon. His anger toward the housekeeper intensified acutely, and he marveled: she was a fine surrogate indeed. Can't a brother get five minutes to himself without being hustled by some faction or other? The lyrics of a crappy ditty cavorted in his head: *Where's a brother gonna find peace in Winthrop? / Shuttle bus shuttle bus shuttle bus.* The backup singers sashaying, hips a-rocking here and there.

The only thing that salvaged his meeting with the reporter was the sight a few minutes later of the DO NOT DISTURB sign on the door of his room. He crept inside. His room remained unmolested. It was starting to look like home in there, messy and dim. A whiff of something sour.

He was going to take a nap when he noticed the housekeeper's second note. This one was more economical. It read, "You THINK you are so smart, smarty-pants. But you ARE NOT."

He scrambled under the covers. Shuttle bus, shuttle bus, shuttle bus.

. . . .

The first time he saw one of the ads he was watching prime-time television. One of the ensemble dramas in the top ten, a show they all agreed on. The commercial opened onto a middle-class suburban kitchen, the kind made totemic in previous commercials, with a little window with yellow curtains above the sink, through which he could see the backyard and the wood fence that kept the neighbors away. A white mother stood with a dishrag in her hand and a white child (Shade # A12) ran in. He looked up abjectly and said, "I hurt." Then they cut back to the shot of the kitchen, but this time there was a black mother standing there with a dishrag. A black son (Shade # A25) ran into the kitchen and said, "I hurt." The scene was repeated with an Asian kid (Shade # A17), again with the identical setting and physical movements. "I hurt." Then came a shot of a white maternal hand fixing white Apex on a white child's forearm, black maternal hand, etc. Then shots of the mothers holding their children's smiling heads to their aprons as the tagline manifested itself on the screen and wafted through the speakers: Apex Hides the Hurt.

You couldn't escape the commercials. Pretty soon the tagline became a universal catchphrase in the way that these things happen. People could take it out of the box and apply it to all manner of situations. Why ya drinking so much Larry? Hides the Hurt. What were you doing on the couch with the babysitter, Harry? Just Hiding the Hurt, honey. The subterranean world of novelty T-shirt manufacture took note and soon ribald takes on the slogan appeared on 50-50 cotton-poly, filling the shelves of tourist traps and places surly teenagers might wander. On the late-night talk shows, there was at least one Hides the Hurt punch line per week. Everybody laughed as if it were the first time they had heard it.

But what was a name and an ad hook if it didn't move the product? The product moved. The boxes didn't say Sri Lankan, Latino, or Viking. The packages spoke for themselves. The people chose themselves and in that way perhaps he had named a mirror. In pharmacies you started to see *that motion*—folks placing their hands against the box to see if the shade in the little window matched their skin. They gauged and grabbed the box, or moved to the next and repeated the motion until satisfied. And Apex stuck. Once you went black you didn't go back. Or cinnamon or alabaster for that matter. Stuck literally, too. They finally fixed the glue.

In the advertising, multicultural children skinned knees, revealing the blood beneath, the commonality of wound, they were all brothers now, and multicultural bandages were affixed to red boo-boos. United in polychromatic harmony, in injury, with our individual differences respected, eventually all healed beneath Apex. Apex Hides the Hurt.

"Isn't it beautiful?" he would ask, as he wrapped up the story of Apex. He meant the bit about the multiculture, skinning knees on some melting pot playground. Hey man, it was this country at its best. They were all stones gathered in a pyramid. And on top—well he didn't have to draw a map, did he?

He never did meet the guy who came up with the tagline, just like he never met the guy who came up with the idea. They were individual agents in a special enterprise and there were no Christmas parties for people like them. They didn't get together but they still knew each other. They kept this place running.

. . . .

Riverboat Charlie's had neglected so many branding opportunities that he wasn't sure whether to blame a lack of imagination or to applaud that quality, so rare these days, of understatement. As he waited for the mayor, he rhapsodized over what might have been. Menus and signage employing the colorful argot of wharf rats and gamblers, a decor artificially wizened to simulate exposure to dark and churning water, a mascot-spokesman in the form of a cartoon character or elderly gentleman of stylized appearance. Under his attention, the humble establishment became a vacuum, and all the outside marketing world rushed in to fill every inch and corner, wherever a jubilant little branding molecule might find some elbow room. He was the outside world come inside to bully about.

The waitress led him toward the back, then suddenly

altered course halfway into the room, dropping the menus on a table for two by the window overlooking the river. At first he blamed his limp, and the waitress's desire to minimize her exposure to his infirmity. Then he recognized the make of the table—it was a Footsie, familiar to him from when the name won an Identity Award a few years ago—and he realized she was trying to help the mayor out by hooking her up with a romantic spot.

He took in the evening traffic while he waited. During his walks around town, he'd limited his patrol to the square, never venturing down the promenade. True, the rain had hampered his investigation of the area, but it was a fact that he was not a very curious man. Riverboat Charlie's was off the main drag, however, giving him a good look at the small pier. It was the first cloudless night of his stay, and people were out enjoying the fine weather. In all likelihood, the building at the foot of the pier had been a warehouse at some point, used by Winthrop to ship his barbed wire out of town, but it had been cut up into tiny shops since. Video store and trinket store and a bicycle shop. At one point it had served a single purpose, served its master. Sure, back in the day, you controlled something like that dock and you called the shots.

Regina materialized across from him before he knew it, preventing any momentary dithering over the right greeting. Hug, cheek peck, or handshake. She was more relaxed this time around, wearing a low-cut blouse that was more daring than he'd given her credit for. "Glad I called ahead," she said.

In only a few minutes, the place had almost filled up. He recognized a good number of the other diners from the hotel. Riverboat Charlie's was probably listed as an approved restaurant in the Help Tour Information Packet, after a list of where to change currency in this strange land and the number of the nearest embassy. "It's never this packed," she added, "unless it's someone's birthday or a holiday or Valentine's Day."

"This is the big weekend."

"They get bigger every year," she said, cocking her head dismissively. "I hadn't thought of the timing when we talked about bringing you here, but I'm sure Lucky had it all planned out."

"He puts on a good show."

The waitress parked a thigh against the Footsie, and she and Regina caught up briefly before she took their drink order. He couldn't tell if Regina was a regular, or if this was standard mayoral interaction. The waitress gave him a snaggletoothed smile before scampering to the kitchen counter.

"Back where I'm from," he said, "if you're a local celebrity, they tape your 8 × 10 picture over the cash register."

Regina gave him a wry look, then gave in. "I don't know about celebrity, but I am a strange creature around here, I'll give you that. First black mayor since we started having mayors in this town. Descended from the first families. Oh, I left for a time," she said, shifting gears, as if afraid he'd think her a hick. "For a good many years. Went away to college. Got married. Got divorced. But I came back. Which puts me in with Lucky. We tried other places, but we chose to come back home. Which means something to people in a town like this."

She asked him about his meeting with Albie, which turned into a long discussion over whether or not Albie was mentally disturbed. Regina was more forgiving of eccentricity than he was. A mom and dad steered their two young children toward a booth in the back, the father offering a throaty, "Hel-lo, Regina," as he passed. The man took quick measure of him, then winked at her. The two kids bounded into the booth with gusto and started flapping their menus in the air.

All this winking and weird glances. She must be kinda hard up, he thought. He wondered if this was the type of place where everybody was related. Where everyone was some degree of cousin. Did that family come from hearty founder stock, were they Goodes or Fields or another, less famous First Family? Or did they move here recently, to work for Lucky or other new computer businesses?

Regina stirred her wine spritzer distractedly. "They think we're on a date," she said. "It doesn't happen that often." She chuckled. "My ex-husband came to town once. Nobody knew who he was. They thought we were having a romantic outing.

Mayor Goode and her new beau. We laughed. Enough time had passed that we could laugh together again." Her shoulders relaxed. "He was a bit of an asshole, to tell you the truth," she added in a rush, and he could see she was momentarily embarrassed by the vulgarity.

He smiled. Maybe not hard up. Just dosed with Isolatrum in the same amount as everyone else. The government was putting it in the drinking water these days along with fluoride.

She said, "People look at me and they see what they want to see. Black people see me as family, because my name goes way back. The white people know what the Goode name means in this community—tradition, like Winthrop means tradition. And the new people know that I agree with a lot of what Lucky is trying to do and that he and I have been a team, in terms of trying to bring this place into the twenty-first century. Way I figure, I'm a bit of a triple threat that way." She halted, considering the full implications of what she was saying. "Of course," she continued, "after my vote in the meeting, people don't know what to do with me."

Sure, sure. He said, "At some point you were going to vote with Lucky, right? Then you just blindsided him. What changed your mind?"

She started to speak, then stopped. By the fish tank, a table filled with Help Tourists hit a raucous patch and distracted him. This Nordic guy stabbed the air with his fork for emphasis. She said simply, "I'll be right back," and disappeared to the restrooms. B for Buccaneer, L for Lass.

The cook slapped a bell, and placed two dishes on the ledge that opened onto the dining room. He had a happy idea that it was their food. He looked hopefully at the waitress but she refused to notice that their order was up. She stood by the hostess station, squaring the corners of a stack of menus. Minutes passed.

What do you call that terrible length of time between when you see that your food is ready and when your waitress drags her ass over to your table with it? He saw Regina emerge from the back of the restaurant. His eyes zipped to the plates sitting on the kitchen ledge. Tantalasia. Rather broad applications, Tantalasia, apart from the food thing. An emotional state, that muted area between desire and consummation. A literal territory, some patch of unnamed broken gravel between places on a map. A keeper, he told himself. Did that mean he was keeping keepers again? Names for rainy days?

She dropped her napkin in her lap and spoke rapidly. "Can you argue with Lucky, really? Can you argue with prosperity? Can you protest change? It's jobs, money for the town, money for the 'infrastructure.' We didn't have an infrastructure until Lucky came back. We had 'stuff that needed fixing.' How can you fight a word like *infrastructure*?"

Regina scanned the room to check for eavesdroppers.

"You fight it by saying: No. Look at the dock across the street. Winthrop comes to town, he has the resources to build that thing. Most important, he's white. What are Goode and Field going to say? They didn't have a choice, did they? Back then. What could they do? They lose this land, this land is what they are at that point. They lose that, they lose themselves. He's not threatening them, Winthrop. But he wouldn't have to say it. They did what they had to do. Give up their name for their lives—was that a little thing or a big thing after all they'd been through?" Her chest heaved but her eyes stared defiantly. "Well, I have a choice. And I choose the truth."

The waitress dropped their plates on the table. Regina took a bite, winced at the temperature. She put her fork down. She said, "Sometimes when I have a hard day and I'm too tired to leave the office and I just want to put my head on my desk, I think about how they got here. In their wagons, all that way from the plantations that had been their homes. Think about that: those places were their homes. Places of degradation and death. So I get my ass out of my office because I have a house that is my own and that's what they fought for, why they came all this way. They didn't know where they were headed when they started or that they'd end up here, all they knew was what they had: Freedom. Which was a kind of home that they carried inside them, if you think about it. When they finally arrived here and looked around, what was the word that came to their lips? What was the only thing they can think of when they see this place they have chosen? The word on their lips?"

For the life of him he didn't know if this was a rhetorical question or if she really needed him to say it. Say the word for her to hear. Also Tantalasia: the in-between place where you're not sure if you should say something, if it is truly as important as it appears to be that you say something, the right words.

Living in Tantalasia. Neither Winthrop nor New Prospera. Nor Freedom. It occurred to him that in its current suspended state, the town was effectively nameless.

.   .   .   .

Assuming you had a facility for choosing the right name, the just name, for healing the disquiet of anonymity through the application of a balming name, you were a nomenclature consultant. He was a natural, they said. During his time in Winthrop, his mind kept returning to one of his early assignments with the firm. It came back to him whenever he tried to sleep.

Statistically speaking, a good part of the Western world has played with Ehko. It was one of the most popular toys in the world. The plastic pieces came in different interlocking shapes, the same four or five hues. Once you learned how to hook the pieces together with that little snap sound, you yourself were hooked for a good stretch of childhood. The tiny bricks were easily misplaced, but the kits came with extras and the prodigal pieces returned eventually, coaxed by brooms, even if it took years.

On the sides of the boxes were pictures of things you could make out of Ehko bricks if you followed the example, and for a while the kids followed the example. Then they found out that the fun part was making their own bizarre creations. Deviating from the blueprints. The toy was plastic and so was its meaning. He figured there was some mathematical way of determining the exact number of permutations, but the overall impression was that there was no end to what you can make out of Ehko. Parents who played with Ehko as children bought the kits for their own children, and Ehko was passed down alongside morals and prejudices and genetic predisposition to certain illnesses.

The march of time. Over the years, Ehko International started stamping out more extravagant sets, like Ehko Stock Car Racing Track and Ehko Metro Hospital. Again, the kids could follow the plans and make a sterling HMO, or stray and come up with their own, more realistic concoctions, like a hospital without a waiting room, or one equipped with a particularly large morgue. The bricks as the very components of imagination. Every year the company unleashed another dozen sets, each new batch more baroque and complicated than the last: Ehko Andromeda Space Station, Ehko Lost City of Atlantis. Made wistful by the cumbersome boxes they hoisted from the toy store, parents wrote to Ehko International inquiring about the simple kits of their youth. One such favorite was Ehko Village.

Ehko Village had been quite popular during the fifties and early sixties. The Town Hall, the Fire Station, the Church, easily replicable from diagrams, addressed innate notions. Something about this country. But alas the counterculture, the political tumult, the odd riot put a kibosh on sales. Times had changed, but the letters from the now grown-up architects of Ehko Village told the corporation that maybe an update was in order. Being Swiss, they had a very reliable system of dealing with customer feedback. Sentiment rattled its cage. Maybe, they thought, the same concept would fly again, if reworked a bit. But they definitely needed a new name.

He met the Ehko team in the conference room and they outlined their plans, these Swiss people. They were a flock of blond birds, misled by the wind to a city where the going rate was mongrel pigeon. He pretended to listen but the whole time he had his eyes on the box containing the new Village. Once they were done talking he told them to ask the receptionist for some tickets to a Broadway show, if they were so inclined. Strip club passes if they weren't. He had his own evening already mapped out.

He took the kit home. How could he resist? The pieces fell in a clatter when he overturned the box onto his living-room floor. The proposed town as pictured on the box was an unassuming thing, compared to what the company had been churning out lately. It was out of step with the rest of the product family and out of step with the spirit of the times. It was no Ehko Boomtown Gone Bust or Ehko Ghetto. The machines, he noted, had not been configured to stamp out the little studded bricks of Ehko Abraham Lincoln Public Housing or Ehko Methadone Clinic. (He enjoyed himself more back then.) In the pictures on the box, there were no shadows in the alleys, for there were no alleys. Everything fit together snugly, and there was no place where an unruly element might find purchase.

Some things were different, he observed, but the steps they had taken to modernize the Village pointed more toward demographic reality than slippery, more elusive concepts. The citizens of Ehko worlds were bulbous moppets with painted smiles; as they did in all their sets these days, Ehko included brown bulbs (that were not too brown) and yellow bulbs (that corresponded to some hypothetical Asian skin pigment) according to ratios informed by sales research. This new Village was integrated. And should a child desire to place a fireman's helmet on a female Ehkotian, it would fit. No longer would pesky perms forbid entrance to the gates of equal opportunity. The shops came in wider variety, and now children could snap an ice-cream shop together or a drugstore. The bricks had not changed, however.

Red white and blue bricks still waited patiently for little fingers to quicken them.

His legs remembered the correct position for squatting down with toys. He played. He fit the round male studs into the round female grooves. He got some thinking done as he hunkered down on his fallen-asleep legs. As he cycled through an array of recombinations, his subversive attempts at city planning, the strangest things occurred to him. Sinister and malformed architecture emerged from the pile, ruins slowly revealed by shifting dunes. He could make out the police station in the rubble. If he left it there, in fragments, would there be no crime? By constructing some sort of fascistic multiplex out of the movie theater bricks, it would, according to his logic, call into creation a new cinema, one appropriate to such a venue, but what sort of films would they be? By leaving out the hospital would the citizens not die? Like the plastic of their flesh and the four letters of the name imprinted on every brick, the citizens would live forever. He could leave out the streets and jam the buildings together into a horror of overcrowding, where no one ever went outside into the poisoned atmosphere, but remained behind the walls of Ehko Dystopolis.

From such a simple assignment, all manner of devilment popped into his head. And of course that's what Ehko was about, he realized. The little children's hands would be like giant's hands, the hands of God, reaching down to the floor of the playroom, building this community and world from interlocking parts, every sure snap sound the affirmation of nature's logic, or at the very least splendid Swiss design. Revoking order only to affirm it anew the next afternoon. The multicolored pieces spread out on the floor like the spiral arms of a galaxy. Which made him universe-big, and he wondered then, what was this toy, and what was this game?

Eventually he followed the instructions. He felt compelled to. In the end nothing was so pleasing as the image on the cover of the box, and this was a lesson to be learned. The original idea remained in that jumble of bricks, patiently waiting.

The kit was still in his apartment, at the top of the closet. He hadn't the heart to throw it away.

They hired him to make the tough calls. He returned to them Ehko Village. Which, he had to admit, didn't seem like a tough call at all. It wouldn't win any awards. Some people, he knew, would say: Well, you didn't really name anything at all, we could have done that. They'd be right, but they would have done it for the wrong reasons, he countered. After Ehko Space Station Delta and Ehko Martian Invasion Armada, a trip back to Ehko Village was a bold choice. It did not need to be updated. It did not need to be renamed. We have forgotten, he told his clients, we have forgotten the old ways. And the old ways have a name, and they have a power. Malevolent imaginings might try to force those pieces into something they are not, but the name will force them into the correct and kind configuration. We are too easily unmoored these days, he said, and the name will keep us tethered. Ehko Village said values were constant, that times had changed but an idea of ourselves still remained. There is a way of life we have forgotten that is still important.

He didn't believe that crap, but that wasn't important. He knew it would strike a chord. The Village was off to the side and timeless. Driving off the main highway one day you might find it and wile away a few hours savoring it. The very name Ehko, after all, what was it? It was what we knew bounced back at us from the walls of the cave, in diminishing repetitions, until it disappeared and we were alone with a memory. So how to stop that? Ehko Village was a reverberation of America that did not grow faint with time. It was always there to play with us.

· · · · · · · ·

True, "Why don't you hop in and let me show you something" did sound like a come-on. Regina's somber mood throughout the last half of dinner, however, smothered the little erotic fantasia percolating in his brain at the sound of those words. As he climbed into the passenger seat, he reminded himself that he had a long-standing rule about sleeping with clients.

Then he recalled that actually he had no such rule, but it would certainly complicate things, especially since she was already involved in a torrid psychological ménage with Albie and Lucky. He shuddered. They pulled away from the curb.

She had a way of speaking that reminded him of his mother and her cousins. And he thought: Is that it? Some sort of Oedipal thing churning belowdecks? First the sexy librarian, now this. He was really hitting the sexual fetishes hard today. Tomorrow at the barbecue there will be cheerleaders around every corner, pom-poms locked and loaded. He wondered about the collective noun for a group of French maids. A stocking of French maids? A garter of French maids? Or maybe it wasn't Oedipal at all. Maybe it was her conviction that he found sexy. He shuddered anew.

"This is all old Winthrop," Regina said, as they turned off the promenade. They rolled past a string of handsome folk Victorian houses. Close to the center of things and nicely porched and well hedged. What kind of view was there from the top windows? What was there to see? Space. This was the trade-off between the country and the city and he couldn't help think: What's the mortgage on that thing? There were rumblings his building might go co-op, so he was attuned.

"This was the white part of town when I was growing up. Me and my girlfriends had this game we used to play when we came by here, where as soon as we got on this street we'd start screaming, 'They're gonna get you! They're gonna get you!' and run as fast as we could. There were all these old, old people on this street and I guess we found them scary."

He said, "Yup."

"Winthrop built the first of these as the factory started to take off, and then he sold them to people who moved here. Once the town got incorporated, it really took off. Merchants started setting up shop, whatnot. Winthrop would sell the houses, and then buy them back, then sell them to new people."

"That's some old-school shit."

"Yeah," she said, chuckling. "But then the last ten years, Albie has sold it all off bit by bit. There'll be no buying it back. It's all Lucky's now, or the new people. I could point to each one of these houses and say, this used to be Winthrop and that used to be Winthrop, but at this point, I think more of Lucky and the new people than I think of Albie and his family. It hasn't been that long, but that's the way it is."

It must be like selling little pieces of yourself. And what would that do to you? They turned off Elm and onto Virginia. "That's probably what made him crazy," he said.

She whistled. "Like I said before, he was always a little off. Like those crazy British princes, the ones that are all nuts from generations of people marrying their cousins. Not that I'm blaming incest or anything. Maybe all royalty is crazy. That's the price after a while." Her eyes narrowed. "His wife was the last straw. I liked her. Everybody bad-mouths her, but she was always nice to me. Took everything but Albie's pants in the divorce, though."

"I saw his house."

"So you know. Yeah, he wasn't right after they split, but he wasn't that right before they split." She pointed out the window. "That Queen Anne over there they cut up into apartments for the computer people. Had a stalking complaint there last spring, so I got to see the inside. They did a nice job with it. The appliances."

They rounded a corner and the homes grew more modest and modern, ranch houses with the occasional two-story wood frame thrown in. "This is still mostly a black part of Winthrop, but a lot of the new people are moving up Reginald Street. Especially lately."

He looked at the SUVs and Volvos in the driveways and superimposed wagons and hitching posts. Were the Goode and Field patriarchs as real-estate savvy as Winthrop? Did they have the same kind of arrangement with black settlers who came later, like Winthrop had with his laborers and whatnot? He didn't think it would be a polite question to ask, even if Regina hadn't appeared to be in some sort of trance. She slowed the car to a crawl and her eyes prowled the fronts of all the houses, looking for something. She said, "You asked me in the restaurant when I changed my mind. I didn't know I was going to do it until I did it. Until it came time to vote." Perhaps she was superimposing her own images on what was there now, placing the faces of relatives and old friends. Her dead.

"I started thinking of changing the signs," she started. "Because you have to change everything, right? The street signs and then the letterhead in the office. And who would pay for it. I thought: It's Lucky's baby, so let him pay for it. It's his, like before it was Winthrop's. It's been done before. And—it was a lie. That's what it is, isn't it? If I ask you your name and you tell me something other than what it is, that's a lie. We got to the conference table and I looked at those two men I've known my whole life, and I thought: This is wrong." She turned to face him, her expression fixed. "It should go back to Freedom. That's its true name."

They were at the intersection of Reginald and Regina. "Winthrop's not the only royalty in town, huh?" he said.

"My brother is named Reginald, too. Maybe you'll meet him and his wife before you leave. Everybody in my family is named after someone who came before. And if we didn't know them personally, we knew them as a place we traveled on. Funny, huh? You get to the white part of town and they named the streets after the colonies, Virginia and Massachusetts and whatnot. Or trees. My mother used to ask me, 'What started that whole mess of naming streets after trees? Didn't they have people they loved?' That's how you know what part of town you're in. Over here, the streets are people. They're your history, your family. Richards, Nathaniel, Goode. How you know you're home is when you see your name on the street. And if you get lost, just look for yourself." She turned right, and he had that heading-home feeling.

Regina didn't speak for the rest of the ride to the hotel, leaving his eyes to jump from sign to sign. Winthrop's Virginias and Oaks were well within character for someone hungering after the connotations of the eastern establishment, he decided. Want to import the coast to the prairie? You have to learn how to be just as dull, name by name. Whereas the black settlers had different marketing priorities. Hope crossed Liberty, past the intersection of Salvation. Better than naming the streets after what they knew before they came here. Take Kidnap to the end, make a left on Torture, and keep on 'til you get to Lynch. Follow the lights 'til you get to Genocide and stop at the dead end. Not exactly the kind of stuff that inspired positive word of mouth among prospective neighbors, unless he was so out of the loop that the phrase "We saw the prettiest little bungalow on Rape Street" was now much more upbeat than it used to be.

What would Lucky's map look like? Take Innovation all the way to Synergy, then hang a looey on Scalability all the way to Cross-Platform. They were almost at the town square, he could feel it. He shook his head: going native. Did it matter in the end what names they gave their roads? There were secret street names, the ones we were unaware of. The ones that only the streets themselves know. Signage vexed Regina, and well it should, he decided. Welcome to Freedom. Welcome to Winthrop. Welcome to New Prospera. Tear the old signs down, put up new ones in their place—it didn't change the character of the place, did it? It didn't cover up history. Not for the last time, he wondered what his clients believed they could achieve. And what exactly he was doing here.

.   .   .   .

One day he stubbed his toe. In retrospect there was some inevitability tied up in said stubbing, so he came to believe that his toe wanted to be stubbed for reasons that were unknowable. Unnameable.

The C-line apartments in his building were renowned for their spectacular troves of closet space, and as it happened he lived in 15C. Where lesser mortals were forced to retain the services of storage facilities, the C-liners rejoiced in walk-ins that but for a quirk of fate might have been additional bedrooms. He reserved two of those uncanny closets for the numerous boxes sent to him from grateful clients. In the boxes were gifts. Or gratuities, more like it. Little tips.

They were things he had named. On the sides of the boxes the names loitered and slouched, matured by design teams and promotional schemes into adolescents with personalities. To look at the logos, his former charges had grown up to be flamboyantly calligraphic or dourly industrial or irreverently trendy. The standard arguments over nature and nurture applied.

Most of the products were of no use to him. Space-age spatulas, automatic bird feeders, piquant ointments in various strengths—they represented the breadth of the world. One Christmas he sorted through the boxes, gift wrapped certain items, and sent them to loved ones. The response was less than enthusiastic and the next year he returned to gadgets and doodads. The gadgets and doodads, like his clients' products, remained in their packages, but he was of the mind that when it came to gifts, it was the appearance of thought that counts.

Of all the stuff in his storage closets, the only thing he had time for was Apex. It was hard to argue against the utility of an adhesive bandage and in those early days of Apex, he, like many citizens, found it near impossible to contradict the reasoning of the multicultural bandage, which so efficiently permitted the illusion of a time before the fall. When he stubbed his toe that fateful day, it was toward a box of Apex he hobbled.

He didn't know what tripped him up. He couldn't remember after all that happened what he stubbed his toe on. Later he decided the specifics were not important, that the true lesson of accidents is not the how or the why, but the taken-for-granted world they exile you from. In all probability he stumbled over something small and insignificant, as is only appropriate for such a shriveled, gargoyle word like *stub*. He remembered going into the bathroom and reaching for the box of Apex. The box was his color; they had seen him in the office and knew his kind of brown. He sat on the toilet and removed his shoe. There was a little bit of blood on his sock, and when he pulled it away, he was surprised that his toe did not hurt more. Poor little guy! It looked terrible. The toenail tilted up out of a murk of thick blood, cotton lint, and gashed flesh. It could go either way. The nail might do a little knitting-back-together thing and heal, or it might fall off as a scab. He didn't care. He put on an Apex.

Which toe was it? One of the shy ones, not the big toe, or the middle, but the one next to the pinky. It sat at the back of the class and did its homework, not likely to be voted anything. Never Best this, or Most Likely to that. The brown adhesive bandage was such a perfect tone that it looked as if he'd never had a toenail at all. That he had never stumbled.

Did it hide the hurt? Most assuredly so.

. . . .

He was fortunate the next morning that his bed was big enough to accommodate both hemispheres of his hangover. He'd wake up for a few minutes to experience paranoid hangover (these people are out to destroy me), then fall asleep and wake up half an hour later way on the other side of the king-size bed, enduring anxiety hangover (if I weren't so worthless, these people would not be out to destroy me). He rolled back and forth across the bed, between maladies, disparate throes, for most of the a.m., ruing his decision to partake of the free shots offered by the partying Help Tourists in the hotel bar. He'd intended, after his jaunt with Regina, to get some sleep. Instead, some of the people he'd met with Lucky the previous night had glimpsed him by the elevators and dragged him over. Then he had been enticed with a special shot-glass version of the Winthrop Cocktail. Repeatedly enticed.

He groaned. Twitched. He couldn't tell if his latest encounter with the cleaning lady had actually happened, or if it had been sculpted from the rough clay of his sundry personality defects. The incident, real or imagined, started with the standard loud statement of intention by the cleaning lady. He did not answer—and then he heard a key in the door. But he could not move, from fear or alcohol poisoning. In his paralysis, he heard the door open—and then stall on the chain, which he had somehow remembered to hook before passing out. The door argued with the chain, once, twice, and then this sinister whisper slithered forth, chilling his soul: "I'm going to clean this room! Clean it up! Clean it up! Clean it allll up!" Then nothing. He woke up on the paranoid-hangover side of the bed, trembling faintly.

Around noon the phone rang and he answered it, purely to test if he was capable of routine physical acts. Caught off guard in the midst of this experiment, the receiver smashed to his face, he agreed to meet Beverley at Admiral Java. It took him a few moments to realize that Beverley was the librarian. He looked for some unwrinkled clothes. Safe from the house-keeper's influence, and under his slobbish tutelage, his room was magnificently dirty, in a state of happy and familiar slovenly dis-repair. It had taken a few days, but he had successfully re-created some of the comforting sights from his life back home, with shirts dangling off chairs and doorknobs, and rumpled pants crawling across the floor. A proper nest. He rescued some prom-ising artifacts and beat it downstairs.

"I said I'd call you if I found anything, so here it is," she said. She slid a cardboard box across the stainless steel counter. A red ribbon embraced the box, tight and vivid against the an-cient cardboard. Outside on Winthrop Square, residents and Help Tourists strolled in the proud afternoon. The weather had cleared up for the barbecue. He didn't put it past Lucky to bribe whole weather systems, swapping favors for stock.

Beverley tapped the box. "Back in '37," she said earnestly, "George Winthrop commissioned Gertrude Sanders to write a history of the town."

He told her he had a copy of it already.

"You don't have this one," she said, rolling her eyes. "Her

first draft wasn't ass-kissy enough, so they made her change a lot of it. The one they published was the happy-face version. I went through this," she said, running a fingertip across the box, "when I was doing the research for Lucky. There's some cool shit in it. Not a lot of juicy scandals, but the old bird really had a way with primary sources. I respect that."

His tongue felt two times too big for his mouth. He took a sip of coffee and knew the caffeine was going to render a harsh indictment to his system when it kicked in. Well, it was nice of her to go to all that trouble. He told her so.

"You're going to like it," she assured him. "Remember when you asked why they put the law about naming on the books? I think it was for protection. It was the second law they made. You know what the first one was? That you need a majority on the city council to do anything. They thought it would always be the same way—the two of them on one side, and Winthrop on the other. They thought they could control him."

"We know how that worked out," he said.

Beverley's lipstick, the barrette in her hair, were the same shade as the ribbon on the box. He imagined a whole store, a five-and-ten, that sold everything you might need in the exact same color: sheets, toothbrushes, pots and pans, lamps. The store cut up into a blue section, a yellow section, etc. The orderly and color-coded world. Then he realized he was thinking of Outfit Outlet gone amok.

"Nice interview in the paper," she said. "Didn't know you were such a fan of Aberdeen."

"Shit." He'd forgotten.

"But then, who knew Jurgen was a reporter? When I worked at Aberdeen, he was this scrawny surfer guy who worked in the PR department. Always playing those first-person shooter tournaments after hours, when everybody went home."

Fighting instinct, he asked her, "What was it like?"

"A press release for Lucky, but everything they run in that paper is like that. It's a company town. That was the fifth time I've read that article—no offense—though each time there's a new hook, or person they're interviewing." She tapped his arm. "You came off great. It made your job sound really interesting. Names are important," she said, and for the hundredth time he was given a secondhand version of a public radio piece from last year, a behind-the-scenes look at the naming of a new kind of hubcap.

Most people had first heard about his profession from that piece, which had been strong-armed into existence by the PR wing of Montgomery-Tilt, just after they started an in-house nomenclature department. There were two things that people remembered about the radio piece, months later. The first was the famous nomenclature shaggy-dog story about the car company that couldn't figure out why their new luxury sedan wasn't selling in this one particular foreign market. They finally figured out why: in the local patois, the name they'd given the vehicle was slang for—excrement! The story was standard dinner-table fodder for namers everywhere, laying out a central issue of their profession with rueful clarity, and it was a sad day for the entire industry when this anecdote was stolen from them. "It's like Prometheus giving fire to the lowly humans!" as one of his colleagues put it.

The second memorable item was the small bit at the end concerning the names of God. It stayed with people. In carefully modulated tones, the narrator discussed belief systems in which there were names so powerful that they could not be spoken aloud or written down. Pronouncing the true name of God, in certain precincts, would implode one's mouth. Elsewhere, scribbling down the name of the Supreme Being would summon an earthquake the instant the last letter was formed. Or some other calamity in that vein. Such was the power of the true name of God. And G-d, too. In Some Cultures, if someone discovers your true name, it will kill you as quickly as if they had eaten your soul. There were colorful, popular legends about the secret names of demons and genies that, once known, bound them to the service of mortals. They would have to do your bidding, perform feats, grant your tawdry mortal wishes. Genies who adamantly refused to do windows would relent once you burned the proper incense and uttered the solemn syllables of their true names. "Names are very hallowed things," Beverley said with gravity, hoping for a reaction.

How were you supposed to get paid if you couldn't even write down the name on an invoice? Sure, sure, harnessing the dynamic force of a name was central to his work. Freedom, New Prospera. Heck, Apex. People want to get in there, inhabit it, roll around like pigs in a good name. He said, "It's a living," and told her he had to get back to the hotel.

"I'll see you at the barbecue?" She pulled her sunglasses down an inch so he could see her eyes.

"You're going?"

"Everybody's going to the barbecue," she informed him.

Was loneliness a brand? Loyal customers, jumbo size, lifetime supply. He turned to leave and she called after him, "I'm going to need that back, you know."

He hoisted the manuscript into the air and bowed.

. . . .

Soon after he stubbed his toe, the nominations for that year's Identity Awards came down. He was at his desk when Roger Tipple strolled over to his office to give him the good news. Tipple's self-satisfied stride, his gathering smirk, the

quality of light through the windows at that time of year—
these things dominoed into déjà vu and he knew he'd been
nominated in a category or two. The last few years, he'd been
the man to beat.

Tipple shook his hand across the desk and exclaimed,
"You've done it again!" The nominations wouldn't be announced officially for a few hours yet, but Tipple had the inside dope. That year he was up for Best ReImagining and Best
Name for what he'd done with Apex, and the company as a
whole was up for Best Identity Firm. It didn't need to be said
that this last nomination was due in no small part to his hard
work on numerous company accounts. Nor did it need to be
said that two subclauses in his contract had just kicked in, and
come bonus time he'd be a happy man. Tipple pumped his
hand again.

He leaned back in his chair. To be recognized as the best
in your field. What name do we give to that feeling?

Apex.

He worked at half speed the rest of the day, which meant
he was still lapping his colleagues. Sometime after lunch he decided *Loquacia* fit the new anti-shyness drug. He'd just started
seeing Bridget, and he called her to tell her the good news, but
stopped short of inviting her to the awards ceremony, as it was
four weeks away and he didn't know if he would still be seeing
her at that point. Occasionally he'd look up from his desk and

catch someone looking at him from out there in the cubicle badlands—Tipple was making the rounds, spreading the word. An e-mail came down from on high, telling them to meet in the conference room at four o'clock. There wouldn't be anyone left who didn't know the good news at that point, but they'd sip champagne from the paper cups with well-manufactured gusto. At four o'clock he took a step toward the door of his office and stubbed his toe on the leg of his desk.

The toe. The toe had been stubbed, and stubbed well. In the days following his accident he learned an astounding fact. Apparently the toe had been strangely magnetized by injury so that whenever there was something in the vicinity with stubbing polarity, his toe was immediately drawn to it. His toe found stub in all the wrong places, tables and chairs of course, but also against curbs, stools, against imperfections in the sidewalk that made him trip but left no visual evidence when he looked back, as passersby chortled. Even through the thickest shoes, excruciating vibrations harassed the sad little digit. He began to loathe low perpendiculars. When he stubbed his toe while stepping into the shower, a thin ribbon of blood snaked from beneath the Apex bandage for a few seconds and then disappeared into the drain. It was blood from an invisible wound. He decided his toe had developed an abuse pathology, and kept returning to the hurt as if one day it would place the pain in context, explain it. Give it a name.

As a consequence, he was in some agony, and hadn't noticed that he'd started to favor his other foot until he got to the conference room and Bart Grafton asked him, "What's up with your foot, man?" Grafton told him he'd been limping for the last few days. He responded that it was nothing. A few minutes later, after Tipple delivered the news to the assembled, his co-workers cheered him, and he mustered a smile. The champagne fizzed in the paper cups. The paper cups were part of an enchanted supply that never ran out, replenishing itself underneath the kitchen counter between festive office gatherings.

They were good times.

. . . .

When he got back to his room, he watched half a sitcom, beat off, took a shower, and removed the sarcophagus lid from the unabridged "A History of the Town of Winthrop." Sounded more like a subtitle. Which begged the question.

He didn't know what he was after. This version lay differently on the page. There were more quotes from residents, excerpts from diaries, and newspaper stories. Assorted herbs and spices, but nothing besmirching the good name of the book's benefactor. More of a redirecting of the spotlight. Only room for one on this dais. If the history of the town Winthrop became the chronicle of the family Winthrop, well, they were the ones forking over the dough. With historians and grocery clerks, the customer is always right.

His flipping-around stalled when he came across a reference to the Light and the Dark, his favorite dynamic duo founding fathers. He shook his head once more at their crummy nicknames. The top of the paragraph revealed Miss Gertrude Sanders to be rooting through the private diary of one Abigail Goode, daughter of Goode the Elder, aka the Light. He loaned the young correspondent Regina's face, picturing her in an olde-timey photograph, tinted in long-suffering sepia. Later, he read, she became the principal of the "colored school" in town. Another dutiful daughter in the clan. Abigail, Regina. Deep in that Goode DNA, a certain hardwired rectitude bided its time. He realized that he hadn't met any descendants of Field. Had he traveled on any streets named for him or his descendants? He'd ask Regina later.

Young Abigail was the main source for Gertrude's descriptions of the migration from the South. The Goodes, the Fields, and twelve other families lighting out for the territories, 1867. In Abigail's account, her father came off as the optimist-prophet type, quick on the draw with a pick-me-up from the Bible and a reminder of their rights as American citizens. Uncle Field turned out to be the downer-realist figure, handy with a "this stretch of the river is too treacherous to cross" and an "it is best that we not tarry here past sundown." His perspective may have been overcast, but from the diary, it seemed that Field had a knack for being right. The Lost White Boy Incident was a good example.

The actual story of the Lost White Boy Incident was very short, but it intersected with what must have been constant concerns for the settlers—where to bunk down, how much to interact with white communities—as well as one particular issue of singular vexation that was timeless, whether it was the 1860s or the 1960s: how to keep white folks from killing you.

The pilgrims were near the end of their journey, a mere few days' travel from Freedom. They set up camp for the night, having passed enough people on the road to know they were near a large settlement. Had it been earlier in the day, they would have sent one of their more "fair"-skinned companions, White Jimmy, to pick up supplies. (One of the group's rules seemed to be: When in doubt, send the light-skinned guy.) Night, however, was quick on their heels. They decided against it. Then the Lost White Boy strolled into camp.

He imagined a cherub out of an Apex commercial: scuffed up, out of sorts, offering up a tiny wound and a low, plaintive "I hurt." The ensuing back-and-forth must have been very contentious. Where did he come from? they asked. What did he want? they asked. Do we have to adopt him? they wondered. How are we going to keep from being killed once white people find him here? Quite the head-scratcher. The little boy, Abigail wrote, was "mute as a spruce." He blinked every once in a while, but it didn't sound like the kid was giving up anything else. If he'd been there, his suggestion would have been to wait a while, and hope the Lost White Boy would wander off again. The sight of the occasional errant roach in his apartment engendered the same caliber of response.

Abraham Goode and William Field were summoned from their no doubt caliph-worthy tents. Solomon time. Goode was of the mind that they had a moral duty as Christians and Americans to help him. A modern translation would be something along the lines of, "We shall return this child to the proper authorities." In response, Field offered (again in the contemporary idiom), "I think we should point this kid toward the woods and tell his skinny little ass to keep walking," being of the firm opinion that no amount of explaining was going to keep the Man from bringing his foot down on their collective necks. And just to be safe, the best thing to do would be to pack up and put as much distance between them and him, ASAP.

Now, the Light and the Dark probably commanded their own zones of influence in the camp. He recognized them as a common business pair: a marketing, vision guy teamed up with a bottom-line, numbers guy. You knew what to expect when you knocked on their doors. Upbeat spin on next year's earnings outlook? Stop by Goode's office on your way back from break.

Wondering if you dare remodel the kitchen next spring? Field will be happy to warn you off, advise you to stick to Cancún for your next big splurge. The homesteaders, he reckoned, sided with Goode or Field depending on what kind of day they were having. Odds were, when the final numbers were tallied, Goode won more arguments than he lost, because he sided with optimism. You didn't pack up all your shit and trek halfway across the country unless you had a strong optimistic streak. That was the Goode part of you. The Field part of you told you to make sure you brought your shotgun. Musket, whatever.

The more he thought about it, still faintly hungover in his upstairs warren in the Hotel Winthrop, the more the Lost White Boy Incident resonated. These homesteaders had escaped servitude and violence and resolved to put it all behind them. Left that misery at their backs to start their new black town, with their own rules. Whites had their names for what they cherished; these explorers, in their new home, would put their own names to things. Way he saw it, the Lost White Boy, in his slack-jawed, speechless mystery, tapped into this key moment where they had to decide if they were going to continue to deal with the white world, or say: You go your way and we'll go ours. Decide what exactly was the shape and character of the freedom they had been given.

White Jimmy rode off with the boy in the direction of town.

An hour later as they packed up to flee their camp, White Jimmy told them that the mission had gone well. Until, that is, the merchant asked the boy what he'd been up to the last few hours, it being known around town that the kid had wandered from his parents' farm that morning. And the kid popped his thumb out of his mouth, pointed it at Jimmy, and said his first words: "The niggers found me." "As fair-skinned as Jimmy was," Abigail wrote, "he was as burr-headed as the most Ethiopian among us." He hightailed it out of the store. The homesteaders loaded up what they could and were on the road "with great alacrity," as Abigail put it. "When we looked back, all the horizon was lit up as if by a giant bonfire. We knew they had set fire to what remained at our camp, and had we tarried, we would have been ash." There was always that kindling problem of being black in America—namely, how to avoid becoming it.

Days later, they were here. In Freedom. So to speak. There were many lessons to be drawn from that story, not to mention a moral or two. That afternoon, he settled on one: Listen to the Dark. He was warming up to this Field character. The man had his head on straight.

The phone rang, and for the second time in a week he was talking to Roger Tipple. His old boss wanted to see how he was doing.

"Lemme guess. New Prospera—Albert Fleet, right?"

"On the money. He's had a really good run this year."

Tipple knew he viewed Albert as a plodder. "How do you like it?"

He heard some ruckus in the background. "Sounds busy for a Saturday."

Tipple sucked his teeth. "Got our nuts in a vise on this Saintwood Farms thing. These new kids we're hiring these days, I don't know." He sounded genuinely nostalgic. "I've missed your joi de vivre and brilliant aperçus. That's why I called—to make it clear that your job is still waiting for you whenever you want it. And also to underscore that Lucky is a very important client, and if you hook him up, we might even be able to get your old office back."

"You're just coming out and straight-up bribing me?"

"Bribe, shmibe, I'm telling it like it is."

"What about, 'Always be true to the product'?"

"Wise up—you *are* the product." Tipple paused to let this apparently obvious concept settle in. "You know you're the motherfucking man, man. Nothing wrong with hearing it out loud, is there?" The edge in his voice eased. "Bert Nabors is in your digs now, but he'll understand if we tell him to move. He's having problems at home, affecting his work, whatever. You should also know that we've thrown out the whole voucher system. Top dogs get unlimited car service weekdays. To work, from work, it's all cool."

He was more tempted than he cared to admit. Camaraderie.

Perks. The very reason for the enormity of his hangover. Those Help Tourists had welcomed him as one of their own, and he missed that brand of companionship. He got a quick glimpse of the view out his old office window. Surveying all below. Everything beneath him. In a rush, he let out the breath he'd been holding in.

"We're a handicap access building now, too," Tipple added. "You'll be very comfortable."

"I don't have a wheelchair."

"I know. I kid. I kid because I love. And also because I am passive-aggressive. We're not handicap access." And that was that.

It was almost time for the barbecue. He was tugged toward home and office through Tipple's phone call, then drawn out to Lucky's barbecue. Lot of undertow around here for so much dry land. Goode and Field against Winthrop, Regina and Lucky versus Albie. Double crosses. Now Lucky and Tipple allied against him. Too bad Triangleville lacked the necessary oomph.

.   .   .   .

They were in the woods, the whole team. A few months ago, Tipple had called him into his office to see if he had any thoughts pro or con re: a company-wide retreat to foster brotherhood, teamwork, any number of productivity-boosting notions. He must have been distracted because instead of making a slur, he merely shrugged, which was interpreted as support, and now they were in the woods, a few acres from a pig farm. Occasionally the wind brought the stench over.

From what he could glean, extrapolate, or otherwise mischievously fantasize from the brochure, Red Barn Retreat had been a successful dairy operation some years ago. Then it passed into the hands of heirs who had few kind words to say about farming, and the whole joint was overhauled. The milking equipment sold to the highest bidder, the livestock hustled into vehicles and obscure futures. The exteriors of the buildings were preserved for the feelings of country purity they engendered in the hearts of visitors, while the interiors were chopped up into spaces more appropriate for corporate workshops. The new cattle the place attracted grazed on inadequacy. It was hoped that after a stay at Red Barn—two to seven days, depending on the severity of the situation—the visitors might have learned a different diet, one rich in the nutrients that promoted thinking out of the box and team-playering. It was hoped that all would leave better cows.

Attendance at Red Barn that weekend was mandatory, but everyone knew better than to expect him to participate in the weekend's activities. He would not repeat the words of the Actualizing Consultant they brought in for the weekend. He would not close his eyes, fold his arms across his chest, fall back, and trust that one of his colleagues would catch him. He was performing spectacularly, and no one was going to make him do anything that might jinx that. Tipple or one of the other managers might have entertained the thought that he'd step in here or there to help out the guys, lend the gift of his experience, but he made it clear from the outset that he would not stray from the sidelines. His names were all the example he was willing to offer.

He spent a lot of time avoiding assorted props. In this room, there were boxes of Kleenex for the inevitable weeping, and then down the hall he'd find straw floor mats, to facilitate the cross-legged confessions about damage inflicted during childhood. Foam weapons lined the walls of the gymnasium, for safe discharge of gladiatorial aggression. It was not clear to him why those assorted clubs and maces were kept behind glass, under lock and key.

That first night he went straight to his room and hid there all night. He thanked God that he got his own room. He had imagined, as they filed onto the bus that ferried them from the city, some sort of summer-camp arrangement of rowed bunk beds. It was enough that he had to work with these people. He was not interested in what they said in their sleep.

He heard his colleagues rise, rinse, gobble breakfasts. To kill time before they left on their first confidence-building exercise of the day, he changed the Apex on his toe, which at this point was a grisly sight. The daily, sometimes hourly stubbings had taken their cruel toll, and this morning the nail came off with the adhesive bandage, glued fast by dried blood. As he watched, fresh blood seeped up out of the skin. Had Apex been a little more poorly manufactured, it would have slipped off in the shower or in a sock and he would have been aware of the horrible transformation going on under there. Had Apex been shoddier, he would have changed it sooner, but the adhesive bandage looked as fresh as the day he had put it on. The wound had been leaking blood, pus, whatever, but it had all been sopped up by the bandage. His colleagues were out in the hall, or else he would have cleaned out the wound right then. He made a mental note to swab it with antiseptic later. He put a new Apex on the injury. It looked good as new.

When the door to the meadow slammed shut for the last time, he figured the coast was clear and decided to venture out for a walk. Then through the kitchen window he saw the junior staff jog by, shirts off, commanded by this type-A character with a megaphone. They were chanting something, but he couldn't make it out. More time to kill. He prowled the plant and eventually found himself in the library, the contents of which consisted of what had been left behind. Mostly business self-help, with titles like *Be the Network* and *The Buck Continues: Shifting Accountability in Corporate Hierarchies*.

Drawing from Red Barn's extensive collection, he

programmed a film festival of five PR videos. Four of them featured the same narrator, a gentleman of bass enunciation. If his voice had been any lower it would have been magma. The narrator of the fifth video had much less to work with, timbre-wise, but the company had hired some real whiz kids for the graphics end, so that made up for it. Apart from that, the videos were more or less identical, juxtaposing heavy breathing over accordion management, value chains, and rightsizing with exuberant footage of assembly lines, shimmering HQs, beaming customers. A thin broth indeed.

The hours passed. His foot—not just the toe, but most of his foot—pulsed with a dull heat. It was hard to tell who the videos were for, whether the true audience was prospective clients or the producers of the videos themselves. Beneath the bravado, he detected a strong undercurrent of sadness. The narrators protested too much, promised too emphatically; the more stunning and intricate the montages, the more exuberant the editing, the more stirring the orchestration, the less he was convinced. Did they believe in their work, or were they just howling at the heavens? Or howling into mirrors? And his co-workers outside, huffing in circles, chanting slogans and credos, what did they believe? From time to time, his names popped up in the videos, and when they did, he jumped. As if he had been suddenly accused of something.

He needed air. He heard cheerleading from the front of

the house, so he exited out the back, catching his toe on the threshold and cursing. It did not take him long to find himself in the woods.

At first it was quiet. Such was his frame of reference that he likened it to the deep silence that follows when a refrigerator stops humming. Only him and the apartment, alone, the end of the fridge's hum the departure of a guest he hadn't even known was present. He continued down the path, which terminated at the lip of a gloomy, mottled marsh. He heard the words of the woods. Animals, insects, small branches disturbed by unseen creatures. The more he listened, the deeper he tumbled into the noise. For a few minutes he allowed himself to be swayed by the sales pitch of nature.

What was it that they were supposed to find out here in the woods that did not exist in their normal landscape? What was out here that was not more readily accessible back home, in his city, with a lot less hassle, with a bright label and easy-to-read instructions and convenient disposable packaging? He ticked off a list of attributes. The appearance of that moss was not ratified by the team after fevered interrogation of focus groups. That frog would not be removed from the shelves and discontinued if it flopped. That pollen was not suddenly hip because it had been seen on the carapace of a celebrity insect. The mating call of those insects was not actually a cover version performed by studio musicians because it was cheaper than buying the rights to the original recording. How pure it all was.

Then he cursed himself. *Nature* is a strong brand name. Everybody knew that. First thing, Nomenclature 101. Slap *Natural* on the package, you were golden. Those words on the package promise ease from metropolitan care, modern worries. And out here, if you opened things up, underneath the cellophane, what did you find inside? That fruit has splendid packaging, it has solid consumer awareness and is an animal favorite. Its seeds will be deposited in spoor miles away and its market dominance will increase. Splendid and beautiful petals are great advertising—the insects buzz and hop from all points every weekend to hit this flower-bed mall. Natural selection was market forces. In business, in the woods: what is necessary to the world will last.

His foot throbbed. He heard the shouting of the men. They cried, "I am an original hunter! I am an original hunter!" Probably they were wearing loincloths. It was a wonder any work got done at all, given the extent of their issues. Certainly this retreat was no escape. Not for them, not for him. This swamp was no more pure than the city they had left behind. He dealt in lies and promises, distilled them into syllables. They were easier to digest that way. But these woods had their own hierarchies and lies to maintain. This place lived on promises, too. City, country: everywhere emptiness sat waiting in boxes, waiting to be opened. Every single thing in his vision was biodegradable. Which was cool. Because 100 percent recyclable material, people really dug that these days.

He stepped away from the cloudy water and his footing gave way. As he struggled for balance, he skipped awkwardly into the mud. He felt clammy hands caress his feet as they reached through his sneakers. He looked down and at the same time took a deep whiff. He remembered that the next farm over handled pigs. Look at him, he thought. Top of his field, cock of the walk: up to his ankles in pig shit.

.   .   .   .

Truth be told, most of the time he didn't know what white people were talking about, but from the references to insourcing and gainsharing, he hypothesized that the two guys sitting across from him on the shuttle bus had just returned from a confab on corporate values. The words they used were strange, odd souvenirs, tiny fragments that had been chipped off an alien business meteorite. This was language from outer space. They wore leis. Some wore more than others, and he gathered that the flower necklaces were the unit of measure for reward. When Jack dropped into the seat next to him, it was impossible not to notice his comparatively paltry garlands. "I only speak when I have something to say," Jack blurted sheepishly. His face reddened.

The final Help Tourist tromped inside and the shuttle bus

detached itself from the curb. None too soon. Everybody was hungry and smelled charcoal on every breeze. The sky was sweet and clear. It was a good day for grilling, he decided, an assessment that possessed the sure weight of universal truth.

Jack pointed at the newspaper and told him that he liked the article. They'd all seen it before he did. He had wondered, as he waited in the lobby for the shuttle bus, why people seemed to stare at him, pinioning him in place, before nodding knowingly. A bit too simpatico for his tastes. He chalked it up to routine paranoia and dismissed it from his mind until he passed the stack of *Daily Register*s sitting by the front desk.

The picture was harmless, somehow capturing his face betwixt outer expressions of inner turbulence—his sundry boilerplate frowns, twitches, and sneers. He looked halfway human. The text was a nightmare, however, headline to kicker. MAKING THE CASE FOR NEW PROSPERA: CONSULTANT VOWS TO "KEEP IT REAL" the teaser crowed, before embarrassing all involved for eleven paragraphs, finally limping away with a merciful, " 'I think New Prospera is a great name,' he said, flashing a toothy smile."

That Jurgen had made up everything in the article was no surprise. Unanticipated, however, was the cumulative effect of degradation, achieved sentence by sentence, detail by horrible detail. Did he really "wink knowingly"? Had he truly "patiently explained the somewhat wacky world of nomenclature consulting"? He hadn't been patient in years, and from an early age had understood that winking testified to fundamental character flaws, bone-deep and incurable weakness. The *Daily Register*. He had not been aware it was possible to subscribe to the very abyss.

Two-thirds of his current client list would be mightily disappointed. He pictured Albie and Regina trading sighs and grimaces with each other, grateful for an excuse to be even more aggrieved than usual. He did not look forward to explaining that no, he was not in Lucky's pocket, as they had suspected from the beginning. First thing after the barbecue, he'd give them a ring. Next afternoon at the latest. Depending.

Jack turned to gossip with another Help Tourist about the tits of the team leader in that morning's Actualization Exercise. Relieved for a few minutes' respite from making noises with his mouth in response to noises made from other people's mouths, he took a gander out the window, leaning his head against the glass. They passed Portasans, bulldozers, and brick piles, symbols to him of condos on the rise. Had that been undeveloped land before, or a place where people used to live? Replacement housing for those who replace. The intrepid pioneers in the seats around him might live in those houses, climb the stairs that were now just empty space, cut the grass that wasn't even seeds yet. This is New Prospera. Move it or lose it.

He felt an elbow in his ribs. Jack confided that he and his

wife had decided to take the plunge. Lucky had won them over. Last night after the square dance—an unlikely success, per the scuttlebutt in the hotel bar—the Camerons walked back to the shuttle bus, fingers entwined, until both screamed at once, "I think we should move here!" This place was magic, they decided. Who cared if it didn't have a name? "Pass up on an opportunity like this?" Jack assured him. "Not again, no siree." Heck, they had even seen a house they liked, a nice ranch house on Regina Street. "It's a little cheaper on that side of town," he explained. "A steal."

Others had been converted as well, Jack confided. Dolly and some of the wives had partaken of the free spa treatment that morning, and in the mud baths someone let slip that they had talked to a realtor. Turned out they'd all talked to a realtor, or rather *the* realtor, as Lucky had chosen one go-to guy for his visitors this weekend. Who cared if he used the exact words and phrasings, couple to couple? The wives were more open than the men about this momentous event, differences among genders and whatnot, but Jack knew for a fact that one or two other guys on their shuttle bus were also taking the plunge. Like they were in a secret club or something.

He had been feeling better, but suddenly relapsed in his hangover and his fingers clambered over the glass after a way to open the window. IN CASE OF EMERGENCY, reprimanded red lettering. He resorted to mentally picturing himself in fresh air, then in fresh air over the town of Winthrop, looking down on all the shuttle buses gathering from all points, from country routes and isolated lanes, for a common purpose. Eventually all the shuttle buses would converge on a particular spot and initiate a reaction.

He closed his eyes. If he had one complaint about shuttle buses, it would concern seat arrangement. On this model, the seats lined the walls. So everyone faced one another. Like a goddamned Jacuzzi. The Help Tourists prattled and buzzed around him. "Lot of single ladies at this thing." "I hear they're splitting the stock next week and that's the real reason for the BBQ today." "It's the cutest little wood-frame house." "That's the guy who was in the paper today." The eager vulgarity of cheer. He kicked his feet out into the aisle. Was it really that bad? No, he had to admit. It wasn't that bad at all. New Prospera—ness stirred and agitated them in a fundamental way. In that deep-down place where true names reside. He was relieved that his client interviews would be over in a few hours. Time to wrap this up.

They arrived, the shuttle buses giant white beetles nudging each other in the parking lot. The former barbed-wire factory was a modest three-story building, covered in flaking paint that had either been stripped and peeled naturally over time, or had been recently applied at great cost. Fashionable design elements hung out in the strangest places these days. The gigantic letters spelling out the name of the previous owner had fallen off or been removed, but rusted ghost outlines remained. Shadows that persisted.

Warning: The Name Remains the Same, But Contents May Have Changed Over Time. A warning sticker equally at home on people as much as things, he thought. There were plenty of people walking around wearing their old names, even though their old natures had been gutted. Happened all the time. Smiled less easily or too much. Tended to dwell on the darker side of life, whereas before. Kinda dead behind the eyes. Presently walked with a limp.

Not seconds off the shuttle bus, he was stopped by Jurgen, who popped up and tapped him on the shoulder. Lucky was waiting for him upstairs.

. . . .

He felt ill and not up to tasks. Not so bad that he felt compelled to visit the doctor, but sick enough that each new activity—getting out of bed, going to work, grunting hello to an acquaintance—had to be prefaced by a few seconds of deliberation as to whether or not he was equipped. His limp was quite pronounced. By now he was certain of his foot's not-so-secret agenda, as it darted toward immovable objects, lunging after collision. He was sweating a lot.

At dinner with Bridget the night before the Identity

Awards, he was not himself. His cupboard of conversation set pieces was bare. Few jokes about world events occurred to him, and the ones that did occur to him were not up to his usual sterling quality. He couldn't bring himself to mention that he felt fundamentally—*off*. In bed that night, Bridget wanted to try a new sexual position, one she had read three articles about that very week. It was this last article that sent her over the edge; everyone was talking about it, it seemed. So they tried. And he was not delicate as he moved to re-create what she described from the diagrams, and he ground his injured toe into the mattress. No, he had to agree, as they settled to neutral sides of the bed, it did not sound like such a thing would hurt so horribly, but it did.

He had a lot of weird dreams that night. When Bridget roused him the next morning, he told her that he wasn't going into work, fuck it. She wanted to know if they were still going to the awards ceremony. She'd been looking forward to it all week, plus her new dress. He told her that he just needed a little rest; he was sure he'd feel better by that evening. "Do I have a fever?" he asked hopefully. She tested his forehead with her palm and tendered her regrets. She left him in her apartment, and he did not permit himself to wish that he'd asked her to take the day off to take care of him. After all, he was not a child.

He took the subway home around noon, steadying himself with the handrail and resting every few steps as he descended into the underground. It had been difficult to leave Bridget's bed. Bridget had incredible sheets. What name would he give to this particular brand of sheets, he wondered—and was at a loss. It was then that he knew he was really sick. He couldn't think of a single name, not even a misfire, nothing. So he fled Bridget's apartment as fast as he could. Which was not very fast at all.

He dozed for a bit when he got home, or at least he lay on the couch and rose after a while, and the time that had elapsed did not correspond to the number of thoughts he remembered having, which meant he must have slept even if he could not remember doing so. His clothes were damp. He wondered what would happen if he did not show up that night. Nothing terrible. Tipple would make an excellent speech—self-serving, generous, and humble all at once. A three-flavor-super-chocolate-vanilla-strawberry-cone of a speech. "Excellence is simply what we do." Tipple sold his success much more efficiently than he ever did. How to get excited about, take pride in something that came so naturally? It was like being honored for breathing. He called into work to assure Tipple that he would make it to the ceremony and limped into the bathroom. Something was definitely wrong with his foot.

Underneath the Apex, the grim narrative continued apace. He peeled off the bandage to moist sounds and released a putrid stench. Twin to the awfulness of the smell was what his eyes told him. The toe was grossly swollen, the skin tight as sausage casing. Every familiar furrow and line in the poor little guy had been filled in by the festering goings-on beneath. A germ convention was under way, or other celebration held by the microscopic and teeming. It was funny, he observed morbidly—the Apex no longer matched his skin. The toe had turned a strange, rotten-apple pulp of red and gray, and there was no community on Earth that might be served by the Apex that corresponded to that color. First thing next morning he was going to the doctor, he decided, and covered up the whole mess with an adhesive bandage. Apex, natch.

. . . .

He followed the blue lines on the wall as instructed. From the lobby they snaked along the corridors, a rerouted rainbow. The red line directed you to IT, the green to HR, and blue to BT. Big Trouble? Tsk-tsking, Jurgen explained that it stood for Brain Trust, Lucky's affectionate term for the exuberant creatives who made Aberdeen Aberdeen. "See you at the barbecue," Jurgen warned him in farewell. Jurgen didn't ask his opinion of the article, and he did not express his opinion of the article. It was understood that they were just doing their jobs. Complaining would have been like one pawn begrudging another pawn for only moving one square at a time.

The hallways were gloomy, stingily half lit in the standard

manner of businesses on the weekends. According to the theory that if you were working on Saturday, you knew your way around. The blue lines bled around corners, crossed other colored lines, then broke out on their own after bridging a conference space or lounge. Farewell, great burning machines, with your vats of molten ore. So long, monstrous cauldrons and percussive steam. The transplant was a success, he thought. The old guts had been scraped out without damaging the remaining shell. He limped past the standard molded plastic of young companies starting out in the world, power strips and cubicle walls, free soda machines and foosball tables. All the Brio you can drink. Aberdeen was merely the latest alien organism to latch on with tiny teeth and grit down hard. He saw the black settlers, he saw pale generations of Winthrops, and now the mouse jockeys as a succession of parasites burrowing under the skin of this land. Transforming it. He followed the blue lines. Furtive and solemn. Downright monkish.

Lucky welcomed him into his office. His eyes adjusted to the daylight. This was the best sanctum yet, nicer than Albie's Gothic fun house, certainly roomier than Regina's car, nosing down nostalgic avenues. Each member of the city council had taken him where they felt at ease, but the sheer abundance of ergonomic furniture in Lucky's office made it difficult to make the case for a more comfortable confrontation. A glimpse of the miraculous chairs and couches made his lumbar region vibrate with pleasure, as they appeared capable of cupping any cuppable part of his body. Three walls were mostly glass, introducing him to treetops. On the fourth wall, Lucky displayed an exhibit of factory novelties: rusted tools of inscrutable purpose, wedges of riveted metal. And of course examples of Winthrop wire, short strings of the stuff artfully arranged beneath a longer string of the stuff that spelled out ABERDEEN. Prickly to the touch, the man's name, what with the barbs and all.

A trophy wall. Scalps. He steeled himself for Lucky's pitch.

"Hello, friend. Are you ready for some barbecue?" Lucky patted his chest enthusiastically. " 'Cause I myself am starving."

"Sure," he said.

"Glad to hear it! Just called you up here for a quick hello. You getting along all right? Anything you need?"

"I've been getting along fine," he said.

"That's great." Lucky nodded to himself and looked around the office. He clapped his hands together loudly. "Let's head on down then!"

"That's it?"

Lucky looked insulted. "You're a professional," he protested. "I trust you to do what's right. Why else would we bring you down here?" Lucky walked over to the closet, ducked his head in, and withdrew a long silver briefcase. He motioned him over. "Check this puppy out," Lucky said.

Instead of nuclear triggers, bearer bonds, or the key to the executive washroom, the briefcase contained barbecuing implements. They gleamed and sparkled in their cozy foam berths, tongs short and long, sauce brushes, spatulas, ornate skewers with odd symbols engraved along them. "They gave me this for my birthday last year. They all pitched in." His eyes misted briefly. He lifted a two-tined fork and considered its weight in his hand, giving the impression that a samurai sword could not have been more magnificent. "Stuff like this makes it all worthwhile," he croaked. "The love you feel sometimes. Sometimes it's almost equal to the love you put out there."

Before this unsettling moment could unfold into true awfulness, it was interrupted by a loud cheer from outside. He imagined tails pinned on donkeys, or battered piñatas.

"We should get going," Lucky said, pulling an apron over his Indian Vest. "Gotta hit that grill." He shut the briefcase and they started downstairs.

He felt disappointed somehow. No complaints about Albie's antiquated worldview, no tortured descriptions of his eleventh-hour betrayal by Regina. No impassioned soliloquy on the spectacular *rightness* of New Prospera. And in the magic treasure chest? Only barbecue tongs and, he discovered later, the special recipe for an astounding vinegar-based sauce, which was folded in a special anti-humidity nook in the briefcase. The man had no reason to believe that the hired consultant would do other than what was expected of him. After all, as Roger had pointed out, Lucky had worked with his identity firm for years. So why waste the breath?

A young redhead race-walked around the corner, flushed and intent. Lucky's face beamed out from her T-shirt. Out of charity, he assumed that the shirt was a promo item from the book tour, and not part of the mandatory uniform of Aberdeen employees. As in the town library, Lucky's motto was cut off, asserting that DREAMING IS A CINCH WHEN YOU—before folds of fabric covered it up.

Lucky raised a hand. "Almost showtime!" It was unclear whether he was talking to the girl or to his own face.

She squealed naturally. "I'll be there in a minute!"

Lucky looked at him and grinned. "I love these kids!" he exclaimed. Then his features pinched together. "And hey, I'm sorry about that interview," he murmured, laying a hand on his shoulder. "It's great to have employees who really believe in the product, but sometimes they get carried away. I take all responsibility, of course."

"Of course," he said.

They were about to hit the outside when Lucky paused, his palm level on the emergency exit. He could hear Help Tourists, Aberdeen employees, and who knew who else making noise out there. He winced at the notion of participating in a mandatory group activity, and hoped that eating would not be contingent on such a thing.

"Can I ask your professional opinion about something?" Lucky asked him, serious for the first time.

"Shoot," he said. He should have known he wouldn't get off easy. They all had the same lot number stenciled on the back of their necks, his clients, they were the same make and model. All of them so anxious to be heard, desperate to be soothed. He braced himself.

"Do you think Charred and Feathered would be a good name for a chicken joint? Like a nationwide chain, big sign: Charred and Feathered. Mascot and everything." He looked strangely energized. "Came to me in the shower this morning. Been bugging me ever since."

. . . .

Outside the hotel entrance, Bridget tapped her foot on the pavement. He was late. He coughed, apologized, and they made their way up to the banquet room on the second floor. She took his arm and he imagined energy flowing through that contact, as he siphoned off her health and prospects. And the nominee for Best Parasite is . . .

He relished the feeling of déjà vu when he saw the doors. The last couple of years, this room had meant good tidings.

Opened half an inch, the doors loosed a welcome symphony of chatter. Chatter—cocktail of conversations, disconnected mutterings, and non sequiturs of dingy social interaction—chatter was healthy, chatter was life, and a tonic for him in his state, fortifying him for a spell. He staggered forward eagerly and almost tripped.

Bridget grabbed his arm. "You okay?" she asked, sizing him up.

"Favorite night of the year," he grunted.

Her palm was on his forehead. "Now you have a fever."

Had he seen her worried before? He couldn't remember, it was all fuzzy. He pulled her hand away from his face and squeezed it. "I'm great," he said, and they were quickly inside the room. Swallowed up. He greeted, was greeted. He introduced Bridget to people who didn't bother to remember her name, because they knew him and knew this would not last.

Eyes dipped to read name tags on breasts. Over and over again, bodies disappeared and people were reduced to white name tags levitating in the air before they became people again. This was a natural law in action. People kept pumping his hand and slapping him on the back and he had to fight back a scowl and struggle to keep himself upright. He imagined termites in his wooden leg. He left a trail of sawdust wherever he went. But no one could see it. He was grateful when it was time to be seated, and everyone scrambled after the tented rows of cardboard table assignments. The calligraphy was quite splendid. Everything in its right place.

Theirs was a small industry and they did not need a large room to congratulate themselves. Even if you had never heard of them, you could figure out the character of each firm by looking at its table. If you had a seating assignment, you were a flimsy metonym for your larger concern. Moniker Inc. pimped all things shimmering and diaphanous and hip. The old joke was that they wrote off their haircuts as business expenses, but he had been surprised a couple of months ago when he'd heard tell of the in-house stylist, and the mandatory biweekly adjustments. Morgan, Franklin, and Stern, the blue bloods, were dressed in conservative three-piece suits that functioned as space suits—bespoke tailoring keeping them safe from the hostile vacuum of a changing world. They were legendary for their political consulting, as the things they came up with occasionally won higher office. Morgan and the other dead boys were up for Best ReImagining, for saving TelKing following the indictment of their entire board for accounting fraud of new, almost supernatural proportion. (Rechristened UnyCom, the company was a Dow darling again.) New Partnership, over there in the corner, served the burgeoning multicultural and eco-conscious market, and the folks at their table appeared to have been beamed in from some politically correct future

Earth. If only their ideas were not as 100 percent recycled as their clients' products.

Panting at this point. He wiped the sweat from his eyes. A jagged thing readjusted itself in his gut. The others in the room applauded as if their lives depended on it. He imagined that all of them had their true names written on their name tags. That would be something. That would be honest, he whispered to himself. LIAR. BED WETTER. These two sitting at Mandala's table, the British firm making so much noise recently. If everyone could see everyone else's true name, we could cut out all this subterfuge and camouflage. The deception that was their stock in trade, and the whole world's favorite warm teat. RO-MANTIC. FAILURE. EMPTY. He coughed and shuddered and pulled his lapels tight. It wouldn't have to stop with this room—what if everyone everywhere wore their true names for everyone to see. Of course it began at birth—by giving their children names, parents did their offspring the favor of teaching them how to lie with their very first breath. Because what we go by is rarely what makes us go. GRIFTER. SINNER. DOOMED.

Mandala won for Best Slogan, for "We Put the Meta in Your Morphosis," which had really helped that new health-club chain get a leg up. The losing nominees marshaled their fake smiles and waited until no one's eyes were upon them. A pale young man walked to the podium and made a joke. Everybody laughed. Witty repartee and anecjokes for everyone. He noticed that Bart Grafton was trying to look down Bridget's shirt. She giggled at something Bart said. He didn't care—it allowed him space for his thoughts. CRIMINAL. WHORE. The man at the podium was named VICTIM, and surely after he received his award his life would resume its natural course of misadventure. Bart Grafton leaned over and advised, "Hang on to this one— she's good first-wife material."

PEDERAST announced the nominees for Best Name— Medical. All the really cool stuff these days was in pharmaceuticals, that's what they kept saying around the office, especially the younger guys, when given a girdle or denture account and cursing their lot. He never cared what kind of account he got. It was all the same. He looked down at himself and saw that he'd sweated through his shirt. Wring it out and watch his fluid self fall to the floor. Bridget saw him loosen his tie and said, "It's all in your head, baby."

He heard them call his name as he slipped out of the room.

FUGITIVE.

. . . .

The last hour of the barbecue, he kept hearing the words "half-price margaritas" in the breeze, as if it were the mating call of a local bird. He'd never seen the official itinerary for the evening so he didn't know about the final activity of the day until the shuttle buses deposited them outside the Border Café. It was a Mexican joint that belonged to that robust tradition of lone ethnic restaurants in the middle of nowhere, beloved by the natives in direct proportion to the lack of competition. The chips were greasy and delicious, and the promised margaritas of a firm, sandpaper variety that smoothed the bristled edges of the brain. Scrape, scrape, shuttle bus, shuttle bus.

He identified that manic vibe common to Last Nights. Last night of vacation, the out-of-town convention, the school year, the summer camp. A distinctive thrum. Look at them, look at them, he marveled. The Help Tourists rooted through the declining hours of their stay in Winthrop, attacking with various success the final items on their weekend's to-do lists. Some of them sought that last piece of evidence pro or con moving here. Others held out hope for a deadline hookup, others made resolutions on how to fix their lives once they got home, unexpectedly emboldened by the simple facts of a new perspective. In the meantime, there were half-price margaritas and popular songs whose lyrics, they discovered in surprise, they knew by heart, even if they didn't know the names of the songs. If only they could carry a tune, he told himself.

Lucky had manned the grills like a maestro, juggling direct heat and indirect heat, lean cuts, fatty cuts, veggies, and patties of different water density and thickness with admirable dexterity. Lucky was a born leader, and a born griller to boot, he had to give the man his due. He'd heard no complaints, and had none himself. The sauce had been especially tenacious, in both aftertaste and residue. A quick look around the Border Café tendered proof, around mouths and cuticles, to its steadfastness, its defiance against untold assaults by moist towelette.

He was not unstained himself, and fit right in. He had made a few new buddies. Tipped off by the newspaper, some of them felt comfortable enough to walk up to him while digging at potato salad on their cardboard plates, or gnawing basted hindparts. They asked about his job. How was it going? How much did he make? These characters were not his usual brand, you might say, but he enjoyed their little interactions. Gerald from Unisol, pasty and pale, who was getting his braces off next week. Lily Peet-Esposito, a half-pint brunette from down South, whose true personality kicked in after three drinks, and who was a connoisseur of jokes describing the cultural misunderstandings that arose when religious leaders of different faiths unexpectedly found themselves on life rafts and desert islands. Jim Lee, who was a lot more hip than he let on, a real student of the culture actually, and liked to time each beer according to a peculiar inebriation system of his, finishing off the last drop with an officious, "That was exactly one hour!" And Beverley, of course, who obviously wanted to sleep with him, patting his arm and laughing at his dumb stories when he was quite anecdote-poor these days by any honest measure. She'd shown

up at Aberdeen HQ in a short leather skirt that had been an interesting if perplexing choice in the full afternoon glare of the
barbecue, but had become, in the fullness of the evening, a most
appropriate addition to the festivities, forward-looking, vision-
ary even, in its erotic promise.

He'd had a not-terrible time hanging out with them that
day. The night before in the hotel bar, too. Two margaritas in,
surveying his new comrades, he had a sudden notion of this last
week as socialization boot camp. An artificial environment created to prepare him for his reintroduction to the world. Work
Task of Some Complexity. Social Interactions of Various Types
and Degrees of Difficulty.

Come back, we miss you. You are forgiven.

All these ragged good times were a sales pitch for
Winthrop 2.0. Honey-tongued and hard to resist. Which explained why Lucky had declined to lay out some elaborate appeal in his office, hocus-pocusing with computer graphics and
laser show and swelling music why he should vote the Aberdeen
way. Everything around him was Lucky's appeal. The Help
Tourists, Albie's bleating, Regina's wan earnestness, the inar-
guable common sense of Lucky's plans and blueprints—every
minute since he arrived had been a rhetorical prop in some way.
From a clinical nomenclature perspective, this was a no-brainer.
These people were already living in New Prospera whether
they knew it or not.

Dreaming Is a Cinch When You Stop to Smell the Flowers. Dreaming Is a Cinch When You Crush All Enemies. Dreaming Is a Cinch When You Bathe in the Arterial Spray of the Vanquished.

He was surrounded by extras sipping tequila drinks, bit players in an infomercial for a lifestyle. All this can be yours for the low introductory price of . . . Were they aware of this? Did it matter? They were used to commercials, commercials were a natural feature of existence, like rain or dawn. Winthrop the Elder had forced his vision onto this land and his people, and Lucky was no different. Sure their methods were different. But their motives, goals, the results—timeless medicine-show shenanigans. Were the smoke and mirrors even necessary, he wondered? New Prospera strutted on the quicksilver feet of futurity. It was progress, and progress was Windex, Vaseline, Band-Aids: pure brand superiority. Beyond advertising. Why advertise when the name of your product was tattooed on hearts and brains, had always been there, a part of us, under the skin.

"Peep This" swaggered from the jukebox, and people shrieked as they recognized the opening sample. Every couple of years a hip-hop song invaded the culture with such holy fervor that it revealed itself to be a passkey to universal psyche, perfectly naming some national characteristic or diagnosing some common spiritual ailment. You heard the song every damned place, in the hippest underground grottoes and at the squarest weddings, and no one remained seated. "Peep This" possessed exactly such uncanny powers, and in the way of such things completely killed off a few choice slang words through overexposure. When grannies peeped this or peeped that from the windows of their retirement-community aeries, it was time for the neologists to return to their laboratories.

Just a few bars into "Peep This" and leis were bouncing off the ceiling. That sublime and imperative bass line, he told himself. Behinds jostled tables and chairs to make more dancing room. Beverley pulled him up. He did not beg off or point dejectedly at his bum leg. Truth be told, like everyone else, he loved "Peep This." It had taken months of brief exposure at the corner bodega before he realized that the song had attached itself to his nervous system. He was more or less powerless against it, a blinking automaton. In the Border Café, he swayed and nodded to the directives of the bass line, nothing too extravagant, but he was, nonetheless, dancing.

New Prospera. New beginnings, blank slates. For all who came here. Including him. No, he was not about to hock all his possessions and hightail it out west, but things would not be the same when he got back home. The old ways would not hold. Would he go back to work, reclaim the mug and office that was rightfully his? His thoughts alighted on his cuff links. When was the last time he had seen them? Where the fuck were they? He

looked around at his new cohorts, into their sweaty, peppy faces.
The name was what they needed. Narcotic. Hypnotizing. New
Prospera was the tune people knew the second they heard it, the
music they had danced to all their lives. That was the point of a
name in this situation: to set up a vibration in the bones that resembled home.

He snapped his fingers in time to the famous bridge of
"Peep This," that dangerous territory that often compelled the
weakest dancers in the room to unfortunate excess, but this
bunch did not take the bait. Which made this a bona fide mir-
acle in process. He pictured "Peep This" as the soundtrack for
an Apex ad, wherein one by one his current co-partiers pulled
back their sleeves or pants legs to reveal perfectly camouflaged
wounds. Slightly roughed up by life's little accidents but somehow better for the experience. He bebopped his head to the
beat. Was he supposed to honor the old ways because they were
tried and true? Fuck all Winthrops, and let their spotted hands
twist on their chests in agony. And forget the lovers of Freedom.
Was he supposed to right historical wrongs? He was a consultant, for Christ's sake. He had no special powers.

He snickered, mulling over what Goode and Field would
do in this situation. The Light and the Dark. Goode announces
in preacherly tones, "We are Americans and the bounty of
American promise is our due. It is what we worked for, it is
what we died for, and we call it New Prospera." The audience

moving their heads in solemn amen and hope. To that sweet music.

He pictured Field, but the vision was dimmer. He saw a lone figure, withdrawing into shadow after delivering a grim, pithy "Where you sit is where you stand." And really, what the hell were people supposed to extract from that?

The song ended. The librarian tickled him under his ribs and beat it to the bar for refills. Jim Lee appeared, mopping his brow with his T-shirt. There were only a few sips left in his glass—another hour had passed. Jim said, "What do you think?" which in retrospect could have meant any number of things, but in that moment was interpreted as the latest inquiry into the town's name status. And this time he had an answer.

The jukebox was quiet, and he seized the opening, shouting, "I have an announcement to make! I have an announcement to make!" Everybody turned. Jack Cameron excavated a drunken bellow from deep in his stomach. Leis slapped his face, hurled from all points. An inexplicable brassiere zipped by.

So encouraging. These people understood him. He would deliver his ruling and be done with it. His ticket back home. "Okay, okay! People have been asking me all night if I have come to a decision. About the whole name thing. Well, I have." He put a hand on Jim Lee's shoulder and climbed onto a chair. He looked out into the room. He cleared his throat. Steadied himself. He met Beverley's gaze and smiled foolishly. Certainly the table was stable enough, and would heighten the drama. So he used bony Jim Lee as a cane, and clambered up on the table. Someone threw a lei up at him and he caught it. He held it in the air and they hollered, one or two among them flicking their Bics and holding them up in tribute.

To be done with his stupid exile. Why had he removed himself so completely from those things that others cherished, with his needless complications and equivocations. It was all very simple, after all. Why did he need to make it so difficult all the time. So dark in outlook all the time, frankly. And he felt like being frank, above the fray as he was, astride the tabletop, on the layer of polyurethane covering the map of Cozumel.

It was a nice moment. Someone should have taken a picture. Nice composition, what with the multicolored streamers crisscrossing the ceiling and his triumphant manic face. If only someone had taken a picture.

He was about to speak when something in him gave way, and his bad leg jackknifed with such speed that he was on the floor in an ugly mess before anyone could catch him. In the ensuing hubbub, he fixated on one exchange in particular:

"What happened?"

"He slipped."

. . . .

He was weak and feverish. Caught in the fangs of the big fear, shaken back and forth. His brain worked as unsteadily as his feet, had wires hanging out after someone ripped out that important piece of hardware. It was cooler outside, much cooler than inside the banquet hall, and this soothed him for a few blocks. The streetlights and traffic lights and neon lights all had halos, and seemed beacons summoning him. But so many different directions: How was he to know which way to go?

He was aware of his body as a shell. Fragile, thin as excuses. A vessel containing the dust of his essential him-ness, which would be lost when the vessel failed. Well, that was the way of the world. For a time he was fixed in his body, stuck and named and fixed in place, but one day that would not be the case. One day only his name would remain, on a tombstone or etched onto an urn, marking his dried bones or ashes. A delivery truck almost clocked him as he stumbled into the crosswalk. Pay attention, he told himself. Pay attention: accidents come out of nowhere to teach you a lesson. He should be looking out for that which strikes from above, things like lightning that fall from the sky to instruct through violence.

Blubbering in his fever. On the buildings the names hung there as if by magic. (The billboards were attached by bolts and brackets.) In the windows of stores they were spread out in an unruly mess, this pure chaos, sick madness, as if tossed into a garbage heap. (Items were arrayed in orderly, enticing displays.)

And the citizens walked the streets, alone, in comfortable pairs, in ragged groups, with their true names blazing over their hearts, without pride or shame, plainly, for this new arrangement was just and true. (Strangers passed him, and he passed strangers.)

Now he was in the Crossroads of the World, as this place had come to be called. The names here were magnificent, gigantic, powered by a million volts and blinking in malevolent dynamism. Off the chart. The most powerful names of all lived here and it was all he could do to stare. He had entered the Apex.

What was all this struggle? He answered himself: There was not enough room to be heard and understood. Every name competed against every other name for attention. (He could not bring himself to call the reward of this competition by its true name, love.) To be heard—because if it was not heard how could it be said to exist? People were always saying, "You have to get your name out there," and in that moment for the life of him he could not understand what those words might mean. We spent our lives trying to keep our true names inside and hidden, because if they were let out we would be known and ruined.

In front of a newsstand, looking up at the sky as if it were a vast eternal mirror, he saw all the logos and names, and saw himself as some brand of mite lost in the pages of the musty encyclopedia of the world. Galanta and Apex, Percept and Rig-itol. If he severed the golden tethers that kept these things close to this mortal world, to their mortal meanings, imprisoned as *products*, these names were the names of heroes who had performed miraculous feats. These names were the names of ancient cities where great battles had been won, where the words *culture* and *civilization* had first been formed by human mouths. But we reeled them in and kept them close to this muddy earth, and on the shelves of supermarkets they were artificial kneecap lubricants, sponges equipped with abrasive undersides, aerosol sprays that magically banished static cling. Such disreputable gods.

Isn't it great when you're a kid and the whole world is full of anonymous things? He coughed into his sleeve. Everything is bright and mysterious until you know what it is called and then all the light goes out of it. All those flying gliding things are just *birds*. And etc. Once we knew the name of it, how could we ever come to love it? He told himself: What he had given to all those things had been the right name, but never the true name. For things had true natures, and they hid behind false names, beneath the skin we gave them.

Constellations wheeled around him, lit up under the auspices of the electric company. He stood beneath them in this mess, limping around the valley of the names. Star watchers were fucked. There were too many stars in the sky to name them all. They were bright and keen, but had to make do with letters and numbers—B317, N467, T675—until they earned their names.

Until then, anonymous and barely there at all.

A name that got to the heart of the thing—that would be miraculous. But he never got to the heart of the thing, he just slapped a bandage on it to keep the pus in. What is the word, he asked himself, for that elusive thing? It was on the tip of his tongue. What is the name for that which is always beyond our grasp? What do you call *that which escapes*?

If he closed his eyes and fell back, would someone catch him? He decided to try it.

THREE

. . .
. . .

H E I M A G I N E D a town called A. Around the communal fire they're shaping arrowheads and carving tributes to the god of the hunt. One day some guys with spears come over the ridge, perform all kinds of meanness, take over, and the new guys rename the town B. Whereupon they hang around the communal fire shaping arrowheads and carving tributes to the god of the hunt. Some climatic tragedy occurs—not carving the correct tributary figurines probably—and the people of B move farther south, where word is there's good fishing, at least according to those who wander to B just before being cooked for dinner. Another tribe of unlucky souls stops for the night in the emptied village, looks around at the natural defenses provided by the landscape, and decides to stay awhile. It's a whole lot better than their last digs—what with the lack of roving tigers and such—plus it comes with all the original fixtures. They call the place C, after their elder, who has learned that pretending to talk to spirits is a fun gag that gets you stuff. Time passes. More invasions, more recaptures, D, E, F, and G. H stands as it is for a while. That ridge provides some protection from the spring floods, and if you keep a sentry up there you can see the enemy coming for miles. Who wouldn't want to park themselves in that real estate? The citizens of H leave behind cool totems eventually toppled by the people of I, whose lack of aesthetic sense is made up for by military acumen. J, K, L, adventures in thatched roofing, some guys with funny religions from the eastern plains, long-haired freaks from colder climes, the town is burned to the ground and rebuilt by still more fugitives. This is the march of history. And conquest and false hope. M falls to plague, N to natural disaster— the same climatic tragedy as before, apparently it's cyclical. Mineral wealth makes it happen for the O people, and the P people are renowned for their basket weaving. No one ever—*ever*— mentions Q. The dictator names the city after himself; his name starts with the letter R. When the socialists come to power they spend a lot of time painting over his face, which is everywhere. They don't last. Nobody lasts because there's always somebody else. They all thought they owned it because they named it and that was their undoing. They should have kept the place nameless. They should have been glad for their good fortune, and left it at that. X, Y, Z.

. . . .

The Help Tourists stood over him, stunned, pebble eyes blinking, before they helped him up. There they were, getting their freak on, and then something like that happens. New Fast-Acting Buzzkillzz—When Everyone's Having Too Much Fun. He assured them that he was okay but maybe it was time to go. Poor Beverley insisted on her aid. He did not need physical assistance, but nonetheless. They staggered down the street and she attempted to draw him out with two jokes. He didn't get either one and unsuccessfully feigned comprehension. His palms were smeared with a mixture of grit and spilled margaritas, a shameful mud.

At the door of the hotel, he gave quick thanks, abandoning her on the curb despite the obvious fact that she would have assisted him to his room and afterward. The night had not turned out as planned for all involved.

There was one more indignity in store for him.

His room was clean.

The clothes folded and tucked into drawers, the flecked cups in the bathroom banished and replaced by cellophane-covered cousins, the paltry lozenges of soap replenished. A lemon zesty tendril tickled his nose. The only mark of disorder was the DO NOT DISTURB sign, which had been rent evenly in two and placed in the middle of the quilt. The housekeeper had placed it just so, the pieces touching at a forty-five-degree angle and elegantly framed by the edges of the bed. A tableau of victory. She had been a worthy opponent, and he lamented this second defeat, so quickly after the last one. Reminded of his misfortune after blissful forgetfulness for a few days, and then bested by a feather duster: it had been a brutal twenty minutes.

He showered, inspecting his body for bruises and marks. Nothing to the eye. Except for the site of his most famous injury.

He fell asleep quickly but it didn't last. An hour later he was staring at the ceiling and he knew he was going to have a hard time for a couple of hours. Cleaned up, straightened up according to the house style, his room was returned to its familiar strangeness, and he remembered his first night in the hotel. Back where and when he started. How had he ended up in this place? Not this particular room, but *place*. No one to call. No one to ask for advice, or even calming nonsense about the events of their day. Sure, he could point to his hospitalization as a clear marker of Before and After, but he recognized such distinctions as counterfeit. His course had been set long in advance. This place was the sum of old choices, the heap of his years. In that nameless town, he asked himself, what was he going by lately? What name was he traveling under? Perhaps his banishment to this place was only fitting. Unavoidable.

His guts twisted on themselves and he uttered a startled groan, cursing the barbecue and all it had wrought. Intestinal

turmoil and insomnia were his buddies until dawn, when he finally fell back to sleep.

Everybody was gone by noon. He heard the luggage catch
on the lip of the elevator, the groups huddle below his window
as they waited for the correct shuttle bus. They made farewells
and traded personal information, some sincerely and some for
politeness' sake, and he was struck by the momentum of end-
ings. Then it seemed only he was left in the hotel, floating in his
bed three stories above the town, a patch of bad weather hovering over things. A brand of darkness that set people who saw
it waiting for lightning and noise.

Things had been reset. Over days he had re-created the
chaos of his rooms back home, and it had been undone. Last
night he had been on the verge of delivering a name, and had
been silenced. By a wobbly table, his stupid foot, a momentary
lapse of balance: it didn't matter. He had been returned to the
day of his arrival. In his new room, he started from scratch. The
housekeeper had made a gift of a neat pile of books in the center of the desk. He reached for Gertrude Sanders's contributions
to the world of letters, the official version and one less so. He
hit the books.

. . . .

Colored.

The sliver of himself still in tune with marketing shivered

each time Gertrude used the word *colored*. He kept stubbing his toe on it. As it were. Colored, Negro, Afro-American, African American. She was a few iterations behind the times. Not that you could keep up, anyway. Every couple of years someone came up with something that got us an inch closer to the truth. Bit by bit we crept along. As if that thing we believed to be approaching actually existed.

It was her use of the word that got him thinking about it. You call something by a name, you fix it in place. A thing or a person, it didn't matter—the name you gave it allowed you to draw a bead, take aim, shoot. But there was a flip side of calling something by the name you gave it—and that was wanting to be called by the name that you gave to yourself. What is the name that will give me the dignity and respect that is my right? The key that will unlock the world.

Before colored, slave. Before slave, free. And always somewhere, nigger.

What was next? In the great procession. Because things never remain still for long. What will we call ourselves next, he wondered. If he knew what was next, he'd know who he would be.

. . . .

People started stopping him on the street. When he went out for coffee. When he went out for lunch, his research material

in a white plastic bag dragging down his arm, dead weight. It began with double takes as he stalked Winthrop Square. They'd gesture at him and whisper to each other, That's him. They
approached, fingers on his shoulder. You're that guy, aren't you? I
know you. Didn't I see your picture in the paper? Lemme tell
you something.

He had considered his three clients, one after the other,
and listened to their arguments and entreaties. But in truth they
were only three of a thousand clients. Thousands. He was quarry
now, out in the open, exposed. If they had an opening, they took
it, blocking his path or looming over him as he sat guzzling his
coffee. The former bookkeeper for the factory, whose posture
was such that he appeared to grow into himself. Teenagers on
skateboards who scraped across the pavement halted two inches
from his face, and cackled excitedly before jetting off. Widows
and veterans with their disparate agendas. Homemakers laden
with shopping. The old white man he had met the first day, the
one with the dog, intercepted him and laid this spiel on him
while the animal gnawed on his shoelaces.

He said, Okay, okay.

In the middle of the afternoon he sat on a bench in the
square. Was he daring them to approach him, did he want them
to? Did he need something from them? He didn't know. When
he caught people across the street squinting at him, he filled in
their backstories. That one descended from the second wave of

newcomers, the ones who showed up in Winthrop when the plant had taken off and was expanding. That lady over there claimed a direct blood tie to those who followed in Goode and Field's wake once word of Freedom spread, once people heard of the place where colored folk could be treated like human beings. Advertising of one sort or another had drawn them here, slogans with their luminous entreaties. Freedom was a place where you could get a fresh start. Winthrop, now there's a place where a man can make his mark. The future is yours. Odds were, if his stories didn't fit the person in question, they were right for somebody else. That white guy right there had only been here for a month, he tapped out code for Aberdeen and was raising his kid by himself, an easier proposition here than in the city he had left. New Prospera was the final element; after that his resurrection would be complete.

They wanted to know what he thought about things. By the end of the afternoon they were beginning to scare him. Better to be back home on the thirtieth floor of a midtown office building than down here in muck, elbow to elbow with these specimens. Giving him the Muttonchop treatment. At lunch he was granted a monstrous vision as the waitress quizzed him, her pen poised over her notebook. Him as the last living being and the rest of humanity turned to zombies. Like in the horror movies. As was custom for such situations, no reason was given for this transformation. Why is everyone so alien? Just because.

He runs through the streets of a deserted town, newspapers twisting in the wind, dumbfounded headlines ripping down the ave. They come at him, lurching, wearing the same clothes they used to wear, normal-looking yet in complete exile from themselves and their histories. Surrounding him, after pieces of him. Hey, mister—what's your name?

The waitress told him New Prospera had a nice ring to it. They approached him and asked questions, as if he could help them. As if they could be helped.

He made some headway. At one point he took a break and found himself by the window of his hotel room. Not looking at any single thing but feeling as if he were peering through the surface of Winthrop Square. To whatever was below. Just spacing out, really, when Albie shuffled into his field of vision, moving erratically down the sidewalk.

Everybody's uncle stopped all who walked by, for a quick hello or catch-up. Almost his opposite number—instead of being hunted, Albie was the one in pursuit. From the window, he watched strollers bend toward Albie's gravity as they passed him. But then, when he pulled back, he saw another level of citizen that purposely avoided Albie. From his angle, he saw them change trajectory so they escaped Albie's zone, crossing the street or suddenly darting into storefronts. Anything to avoid this strange man. It didn't matter what his name was, or how many times a day they said it, wrote it on envelopes, read it on signs.

The old man was weird and unsettling. And that was that. He felt guilty for his vantage point on the third floor, as if he were eavesdropping on people's thoughts.

It was the last time he saw Albie. Winthrop's favorite son. Why hadn't the two freed men named the town after themselves, he wondered. Goodefield. Nice place to raise a family, they're closing the drive-in to open a new mall, and it's about time. Certainly the duo didn't lack for ego. It required a certain lack of modesty to lead your followers across hundreds of miles of wilderness and whatnot, and all the homesteaders in their caravan qualified as followers in his book. He crunched the names, fed them into the input slot of his particular talent. Goode the Light, Goode Delight: a maker of vibrators. Field the Dark, Field Dark: where you find yourself when you are lost. Darkfield: manufacturer of military equipment, ordnance, and such. Darkfield Military Supply. Darkfield Secrets and Enigmas Inc.

On paper, in the official history, they were even-stake partners, but when it came to day-to-day matters, you were going to go with one or the other. The Light or the Dark. You had to pick one, he knew. To give your allegiance to, when faced with Lost White Boys or night riders or more mundane obstacles. How to shake off the nightmare. How to make it through the day. And more often than not, you were going to go with Goode. Sleep came more easily, no doubt, with his words echoing in your head. You understood deep down that what Field had to say was the world's truth, but you were going to pick Goode every time. It was easier that way.

Had he seen any signs around town with Field's name? Where were his sons and daughters? He knew more than he wanted to about Winthrops, had broken bread with a bona fide Goode. Where was Field's legacy? Where were his streets, and where did they lead?

Even before he discovered the discrepancy, he had decided that Field hadn't voted to change the name to Winthrop. It wasn't in the man's nature.

He was eating dinner in Riverboat Charlie's, papers spread out before him. He noticed a spot of coffee on a page from Gertrude's original manuscript and started to wipe it off. These were historical documents, after all. Didn't want Beverley to spank him. Anyway. His eye fell on the words, "Field had taken to fever and was not present, but the motion was passed unanimously and the town was changed forever. Winthrop was born." He'd read that passage a few times already, but it had never registered. Field didn't vote?

He opened up the official, bound version to see how the section survived the Winthrop Foundation editing process. He tried to avoid getting tartar sauce on the pages as he searched out the passage in question. "The motion was passed unanimously, and with a stroke of a pen, the town was changed forever.

Winthrop was born." No mention of Field, ill or otherwise. The final version was richer one cliché and short one local character.

He called up Regina. He had some questions.

. . . .

He liked his epiphanies American: brief and illusory. Which is why he was so disappointed that a week after the operation he still felt such deep disquiet. Pierce the veil, sure, that was one thing. To walk around with the weight of what he had witnessed, quite another. Or limp around, more accurately.

It started in the hospital, the long road to hermitage. Later, he retained a few shadowy recollections of acquaintances by his bedside. Someone squeezing his hand, probably Bridget, murmuring earnestly, "Can you hear me in there?" Or perhaps this was from coma movies, and merely appropriated from popular culture for the occasion of his hospitalization. When he was conscious, and had stepped down from his fever mountain, they gave him the skinny on what had befallen him. Discovered, delirious and muttering, sprawled out on a street corner. Delirious but well dressed, which was why he was eventually taken to the emergency room, instead of being left to rot. The ghastly shock waiting underneath the adhesive bandage, and the amputation of his putrefying toe, no other option at that point. His only response to the news was to inform the nurses that he would refuse all visitors.

Bridget made a commendable effort, expending the energy to make six phone calls and two attempted visits to his room. It was more than he gave her credit for, more than he deserved, actually, and he couldn't help but be slightly moved. That she did not persevere after the first few days was just as well. He would have defeated her in the end. Tipple and the rest did their part, some of them making it to the door of his room before being scooped up by the nurses. He rebuffed them all. This prepared his co-workers for the letter he sent weeks afterward, informing them that he would not be returning to the office. Foreshadowing, he mumbled to himself, as he hoisted the hospital room remote. The remote control was connected to the wall by a heavy umbilicus, and the weight of the wire hanging over the side of the bed kept it creeping away from him as if it were alive.

The doctor was a third-year resident, rendering into dull comedy utterances such as, "In all my years of practicing, I have never seen such neglect." Doctor Miner presented the scenario with a charming air of exasperation. The repeated assaults on the toe's well-being had left it merely ugly, Doctor Miner explained. It would have healed in time. The real culprit was the infection, which had remade the flesh after its own hideous design. He was writing up the case for a medical journal, so startling was the pedigree of the microscopic creatures who turned up in the culture taken from the star-crossed digit. "In all my years of practicing," he told him, "I've never seen such an eclectic group." He rattled off the arcane names of organisms with relish, as if recounting the guest list at the glamorous party he'd hosted the night before.

Retracing his steps proved fruitless. For all intents and purposes, he received the infection from a toilet seat. Only months later, when he was laid out on the couch in perfected lassitude, did he remember the weekend at Red Barn, and his encounter with the lagoon of pig shit from the farm next door. Who knew what was living in that hellish swamp, biding its time. Must have been quite a party inside his sneakers, with an all-access pass to his wounded toe. Served him right for trying to get a little nature.

Advanced State of Necrosis. Good name for a garage band.

"How could you let it get so far?" Doctor Miner demanded. "A guy like you should know better." Which sounded at first like a racial remark, but he couldn't work up any rote indignation. He should have known better.

He explained about the Apex. He hadn't even known anything was amiss down there, apart from the pain from the constant stubbing, which, truth be told, he had accepted as his lot and gotten used to after a while.

The doctor simply said, "Apex," shaking his head in morose recognition. "There's a lot of that going around."

On the subject of the limp, the physician was adamant in

his diagnosis. There was no reason for it. The human body is an adaptable instrument, the doctor told him.

The mind is less so, he told himself.

Hobblon for the Limpers in Your Life. Hobblon Makes Your Gimp Limp Hip. From Stub to Stump Using My Patented Five-Point System.

He adjusted quickly to the recluse lifestyle, which was much more complicated than it appeared to outsiders, who enjoyed their invigorating jaunts outdoors and frequent social interaction without considering the underlying structures holding everything together. Keeping away from people, that was easy. Neglecting one's physical appearance, that wasn't too difficult either. The hard part was accepting that the world did not miss you.

Weeks into months. And so on. He became acquainted with the sadism of time, and then accepted said sadism as an unavoidable feature of existence, as if it were a noisy upstairs neighbor. Eventually, his award arrived in the mail. He never opened the box; instead he put it in the closet with the other cheap trophies, the piles and piles of things he had named.

It was not all stasis and sweet, sweet languor, however. He ended up doing a phoner, a few weeks after the incident. Roger called him up, breaking down the situation with uncharacteristic hysteria. The firm was a week overdue on a lucrative account with a car company that was about to announce their new line of mid-priced hybrid-fuel minivans. The car company knew they wanted "100" in the name—their in-house team had arrived at this after years of feuding, bad feelings, and busted friendships. They were definitely going to stick with 100, after so much bloodshed. The other element—well, that was where Tipple and his old team were supposed to come in.

It was a no go, however. "It's like everybody's come down with some kind of goddamned brain flu," Tipple complained. Everyone was quite put out. Any chance, Tipple asked, that he might help out?

He listened to the story distractedly. He was unaccustomed to normal speech, having grown more acquainted with the dingy dramas of afternoon television, and their dispiriting cadences. The world of afternoon television astounded and delighted in the sheer breadth of its humiliations. The streets were filled with victims, and the television programs sought them out for the delectation of those at home, whose own deep and particular brands of abjectness could not compete. The signs and symbols were simple and direct. Nothing complicated or duplicitous about them. Nothing lying in wait for ambush. He observed the shape of his body on the couch. He was shriveled into a comfortable fetal pose that resembled a question mark. So he said, "Give them a Q."

"What?"

"Give them a Q," he repeated. He hung up.

He got a check in the mail a few weeks later, but he wasn't sure if that was for merely picking up the phone, or if they had used his contribution. Such as it was. Only when he saw the ads for the Q-100 did he get his answer. A Q. It was a name reduced to abstraction. To meaninglessness. It depressed him, the ridiculousness of seeing his whim carved into the culture. How'd you come up with that? Just sitting around and it occurred to me. What curdled in his thoughts was how easy it was, even after his misfortune. Nothing had changed.

. . . .

He feared he'd have to buckle up for another ride down shadowy sentimental lanes, but they didn't go very far at all. She picked him up in front of the hotel, and they drove down the block, across the street, then on to the pier. They could have walked. The car nosed up to the guardrail at the end of the pier, the headlights draping a white shape on the water for a few seconds before she cut the engine. Couples and kids walked slowly on the asphalt, sucking ice cream and commenting on the stars in a Sunday-night daze. Back to work tomorrow. For a second he'd had an image of her steering them into the drink. For discovering the terrible secret, but of course it was only a terrible secret if anyone cared. And no one cared. Except him.

Regina cleared her throat. And once more. She began: "The thing about him being sick started because he did fall ill soon after, and never got better. He died. So that got mixed in there over the years, but on the day of the actual vote, he was there. Yes." She tapped her fingers on the steering wheel and finally turned to face him, her eyes red-vined. "When can we expect your decision?" she asked, her voice crisp, almost bullying. More sheriff than mayor.

"Soon," he said. "I think I'm almost there."

"No surprise which way you're leaning."

"You know that article was a piece of crap. Just some PR."

"I know," she said eventually.

He was in no hurry. He let her take her time. A hollow clanking sound, rigging animated by the wind, made its way across the water. Ghosts rattling their chains, he thought. Hey, 'member me?

"It's a wonder they were friends at all," Regina started. "They had such different temperaments. What united them was their tragedy, if you think about it. And the idea that they could make something better."

He had pictured the scene repeatedly over the last few hours. Field walks in thinking it was business as usual. Him and his friend against Winthrop. Maybe humming a spiritual or something, fuck, he didn't know. The kind of song you sing when you are about to be ambushed. A Caught Unawares song.

Regina said, "Abraham had a family. And then the extended family of all the people who followed them here. He had responsibilities. Field didn't have anyone. He'd lost his family back on the plantation. You have to understand where they both were coming from."

He thought: They put the law down to protect themselves against Winthrop. As long as they stood together on the city council, the two black men were a majority, and there was nothing the white man could do. They got it in writing, on the books, the way white people did it. And that would be enough, right? So they thought. What name to put to the expression on Field's face when they took the vote? A Jeep made a U-turn behind Regina's car, blinding him for a second. He had to admit that Regina had a distinguished profile. The blood of kings in her veins, nose and brow and chin of the brand that said: We make the hard decisions.

Her hand went for the ignition, stalled on the key, then fell into her lap. "Man," Regina said, "I don't know what Winthrop promised him. Property? Money? They definitely didn't talk about that on Easter or Christmas, when we used to sit around and the old folks would tell us the story about how we came here. How proud we all should be that we were related to such strong souls."

At the very least Goode got a few street signs out of it. He looked over at Regina. What was she hoping to accomplish, really, by bringing the town back to Freedom? To undo the double cross? Right the injustice. Only it was not the injustice he had been thinking of. "What are you going to do?" he asked. He didn't know what he meant.

She said, "Maybe he didn't get anything concrete. Maybe it was enough that it was the most prudent thing for the community they were building. That," she said, pointing at the end of the pier, the dark water, "that was going to make or break this place. Supply lines. He knew that. So why not change the name. Right?"

"I can't tell you that," he said. He'd been trying to get into the heads of those two men, but was having a hard time. They lived in a completely different context. What did a slave know that we didn't? To give yourself a name is power. They will try to give you a name and tell you who you are and try to make you into something else, and that is slavery. And to say, I Am This—that was freedom. He imagined the vote again. Did they come to blows? Did they curse? What name to give to the smile on Sterling Winthrop's face. Jagged syllables and sharp kickers all the way. And what name to give to the lack of surprise on Field's face. Because he must have known from the beginning of their trip that some brand of doom was waiting for him up here. Or not waiting, but dogging his every step, like it always did. His shadow and true companion.

"I wish I could ask them," Regina said wistfully. "I wish I had been there when they first arrived and looked around and said, 'This is the place.' It must have been beautiful. It was

Abraham that came up with Freedom, did you know that? Field was of his own mind, of course, with some cockeyed idea, but the people decided to go with Freedom."

He asked what Field's suggestion had been.

It took her a minute before she was able to recall it. Seeing his expression, she shook her head in gentle dismay, her lips pressed together into a thin smile. "Can you imagine thinking that would be a good name for a place where people live?" she asked.

.   .   .   .

Any handy road atlas describes the long tradition of noun names, adjectival names, that yoke abstraction to dirt, where we can get our grimy hands on it. Confluence, KY, Friendship, LA, Superior, CO, Commerce, OK, Plush, OR. Hope, AR, naturally. Oftentimes these names can also be found on the sides of packages of laundry detergent or abrasive cleaners, so generous and thorough is the sweep of their connotation. Freedom, needless to add. Can't forget Freedom.

Truth or Consequences, NM. Hard to knock such brave and laudable candor. Such ballsy defiance to the notion of salesmanship. Pity the poor board of tourism for Truth or Consequences, NM! Death Valley, too, won points for its plainspoken delivery. Seeming to say: It's not like we didn't warn you.

There were towns whose names were like thieves,

attempting to pick the pocket of history, but instead became punch lines to jokes about the perils of juxtaposition. Milan, MN, Lebanon, OK, Dublin, IA, Brooklyn, OH. As if history came equipped with tiny snap-on hooks, was lightweight and portable and could be thrown up on available surfaces to accent the scheme of any room.

There was also a long tradition in naming places for great men, or at least men who believed in their greatness. He'd always had a soft spot for Amerigo Vespucci, who got lost while looking for the Indies and hit nomenclature's Big Kahuna instead. Unless there was a gent named Europo he'd never heard about.

He couldn't argue with America. It was one of those balloon names. It kept stretching as it filled up, getting bigger and bigger and thinner and thinner. What kind of gas it was, stretching the thing to its limits, who could say. Whatever we dreamed. And of course one day it would pop. But for now, it served its purpose. For now, it was holding together.

．　．　．　．　．　．　．　．

He didn't want a drink, or need a drink, or particularly want to see the man again, but he found himself walking to the hotel bar. His meeting with Regina had taken care of all the mysteries save one.

The place was graveyard quiet, as it had been the first

night. Everything restored. He saw that once again, Mutton-chops presided over his musty realm, wilted rag in one hand for a scepter, old-school Afro his one true crown. As usual, Mutton-chop's face came pre-frowned. When he saw his customer enter, his hand swatted the tap and the beer roiled down into a mug. "You look like a man who's looking for something he ain't sure he wants to find," the bartender pronounced, "or if he does, ain't sure he knows what to do with it."

But he was not going to waver this time, and he held Mut-tonchop's stare. "I have no idea what that means," he said. "I just want to know one thing—do you ever take a day off, or are you here every day standing in judgment of everyone unlucky enough to get thirsty in this fucking hamlet?"

Neither man moved for a long time, the time it took for the silence to relent and allow it to be possible to actually hear the head on the beer pop away, called up into the fizzy hereafter. Finally, Muttonchops withdrew, wrapping his rag around his fist. "I take two days off—my birthday, and that of my wife. People of this town can count on that like they can count on the dawn. Other than that, we're here every day. Me tending to the bar, and she cleaning the rooms. Just like it's always been."

His higher cognitive functions derailed by Muttonchop's statement, all he could say was, "I'm not thirsty," and retreat to his room. There was only so much he could accomplish during his visit.

There were just a few hours to go. He did not rest. For old times' sake, he decided to order a cucumber sandwich. For symmetry's sake. No one answered the phone, however. It was just as well.

As he packed, he had to admire Field for his principles, if not his understanding of the way people live. The man could read a map, read a compass, lead the people out of the wilderness, but he'd never make it as a modern-day nomenclature consultant. Given the choice between Freedom, and his contribution, how could their flock not go with Goode's beautiful bauble? Field's area of expertise wasn't human nature, but the human condition. He understood the rules of the game, had learned them through the barb on the whip, and was not afraid to name them. Let lesser men try to tame the world by giving it a name that might cover the wound, or camouflage it. Hide the badness from view. The prophet's work was of a different sort.

Freedom was what they sought. Struggle was what they had lived through.

Apex was splendid, as far as it went. Human aspiration, the march of civilization, our hardscrabble striving. Brought it all under one big tent, gathered up all that great glorious stuff inside it. But he had to admit that Struggle got to the point with more finesse and wit. Was Struggle the highest point of human achievement? No. But it was the point past which we could not progress, and a summit in that way. Exactly the anti-apex, that peak we could never conquer, that defeated our ambitions despite the best routes, the heartiest guides, the right equipment.

His contract called for his clients to keep the name he gave them for one year. Who knew? They might even come to like it. Recognize it as their own. Grow as comfortable with it as if it were their very skin.

As he fell asleep, he heard the conversations they will have. Ones that will get to the heart of this mess. The sick swollen heart of this land. They will say: I was born in Struggle. I live in Struggle and come from Struggle. I work in Struggle. We crossed the border into Struggle. Before I came to Struggle. We found ourselves in Struggle. I will never leave Struggle. I will die in Struggle.

. . . .

He left the envelope at the front desk. It was addressed to the city council. He gave the white guy at the desk ten bucks to return Gertrude's manuscript to Beverley. Which was a bit of a cop-out, but it was time to get out of town. As he dragged his bag across the lobby, he locked eyes with Muttonchops, who was framed in the doorway of his domain, slowly massaging a martini glass with a brown cloth. He gave the bartender the finger, and picked up his pace a smidgen as he beat it through the doors, clomping along on his bad foot, absurd as usual.

The bus stop was right outside the library. Former library, actually. He waited and listened to the extravagant racket coming from behind the plywood. They must have arrived at dawn, the expert army of craftsmen-proselytizers come to enlighten the heathens. Double or nothing the store would be open for business by day's end.

Over the weekend, an edict had come down from HQ that all COMING SOON OUTFIT OUTLET signs were to be twice as big as before—how else to explain the gigantism of the new sign bolted to the fence? The old sign was heaped on top of a dumpster, cracked over shards of broken bookcases and institutional chairs. He had to admit, the new sign possessed a certain majesty, and would be visible from even farther away. The next version would probably be visible from space.

There had been a moment a few hours ago, as he was lying in bed waiting for the morning to come, when he thought he might be cured. Rid of that persistent mind-body problem. That if he did something, took action, the hex might come off. The badness come undone. He thought, plainly speaking, that he'd lose the limp. Nothing as dramatic as the cripple flinging his crutches into the air before dashing himself to the floor and break dancing, but still. Something, anything.

As the weeks went on and he settled into his new life, he had to admit that actually, his foot hurt more than ever.